# ABSOLUTE INTOLERANCE

## KENNETH EADE

D1521696

Times Square Publishing
Copyright 2015 Kenneth Eade

ASIN: 978-1522752202

# OTHER BOOKS BY KENNETH EADE

## Brent Marks Legal Thriller Series

A Patriot's Act

Predatory Kill

HOA Wire

Unreasonable Force

Killer.com

## Espionage

An Involuntary Spy

To Russia for Love

## Non-fiction

Bless the Bees: The Pending Extinction of
our Pollinators and What You Can Do to Stop It

A, Bee, See: Who are our Pollinators and
Why are They in Trouble?

Save the Monarch Butterfly

For Valentina, the love of my life, my partner, and my muse

"In order to have faith in his own path, he does not need to prove that someone else's path is wrong."

-Paolo Cohelo

# PROLOGUE

Susan Fredericks parked her car in the driveway at 12600 Foothill Road and popped the trunk. When she opened the driver's side door, she was engulfed immediately by the sweet jasmine of her brother's herb garden. It was so quiet, she could hear the buzzing of the bees as they foraged from flower to flower, and the occasional car on Foothill, which was less busy than usual on this early Sunday afternoon.

The property was isolated. It's what Jim, her brother, and her brother in law, Ron, liked about it the most. *Too isolated. I must have told him that a thousand times.* The driveway ended at the separate garage a good 150 yards from the road, and their little cottage was set back even further.

Among her three siblings, Jim was the closest. He had always been different, but Susan had never had a problem with his differences, unlike her other two brothers. Mom had adapted to it easily. She knew he was not the same as other boys. But, sadly, Dad was a little slow in accepting Jim as he was. They would have been proud of what he had become: a successful Internet entrepreneur.

Susan threaded the handle of her purse up her arm so she could use both hands to haul the three plastic bags of gifts from the trunk. Unfortunately, she had not been able to attend the wedding itself, but Jim and Ron had planned a big reception for the weekend. She had flown in from Kansas City specifically for the occasion, and had spent time collecting presents that she thought would make their cottage very homey.

As she walked down the path to the front door through the canes of pink, white and red violet, and the aroma changed to the sweet smell of roses, she felt an uneasy feeling in her stomach. Something was just not right. *Do I have everything? Did I lock the car?* She fumbled in her purse for the keys, turned toward her car, and clicked the "lock" button on the remote. The blinking of the lights and honk of the horn reassured her that it was, in fact, locked.

At the front door, Susan extended her right index finger through the handles on two of the bags to push the doorbell, but she didn't hear it ring. She knocked on the door and, as she did, it creaked forward. It was open. *Jim's always leaving his door open. Doesn't he care about security? Well, maybe they've already had breakfast and they're outside puttering around.*

She peered down the rows of the garden to ascertain if her suspicions were correct. *They're probably out back. I'll just go in.*

The interior was even more silent than the quiet surroundings outside. Susan stepped into the foyer.

"Hello?" she called out. No answer.

"Hello?" she said again, a little louder, as she ventured to the entrance of the living room, a little afraid of the silence - especially since the front door had been left open.

Suddenly she noticed the writing in what appeared to be red paint, dripping letters across the ivory wall in between Jim and Ron's Chagall oil and Picasso sketch. It read: "GOD HATES FAGS."

Susan began to shake. "Jim? Ron? Are you here?"

In a panic, she ran into the living room, inhaled to call out their names one more time, and exhaled a shriek as she dropped her bags. In front of her were two bodies. At first, they looked like mannequins dipped in oil and then wet red paint. They were unclothed and arranged in a Yin Yang position on the floor, surrounded by a large pool of blood, and had been placed in front of the panoramic window from which you could see out across the back garden and pool, through the city of Santa Barbara nestled in the valley, and all the way out to the sea. Out there the hustle and bustle, the dreams and disappointments of life, continued. In here, it had stopped.

Susan strained to make out their faces and she tried to come closer, but she couldn't. There were bloody gashes in the bodies. She couldn't tell which was Ron or which was Jim. *Oh, dear God! It has to be them!* Her eyes blurred from the tears, cascading mascara down her cheeks. The two bodies had to be those of Jim and Ron and they were also obviously dead.

Susan's knees went weak and her legs shook. She felt like falling, but had the urge to run at the same time – just get out of there. The shock and grief were overwhelming; but more powerful

4

than that was her urge to flee. *Is the killer still in the house?* She didn't wait to find out. Instead, she turned and ran, leaving the bags where she had dropped them and taking only her purse, which was still hanging on her elbow. She would call 9-1-1 as soon as she was as far away from the cottage as possible.

# CHAPTER ONE

Brent Marks sat with his clients, James Fredericks and Ronald Bennett, in the second row of the gallery waiting for their case to be called, and his thoughts ran wild with boredom. He also couldn't help but feel a little intimidated: not because he was sitting between two gay men (which some guys might be a little uncomfortable with), but because they were dressed so much better than he was. And neither of them seemed to have the budding spare tire around the middle that Brent had been wrestling with at the gym for the past three years. It was embarrassing. People might think that Brent was the shabby client who had come to court with his two good-looking lawyers, instead of the other way around. His three-year-old brown Cerutti suit was no match for the crisp, clean, brand-new navy blue Versace that Ron was wearing; nor was it even in the same league as Jim's slick, slim black Armani. Brent could never understand how a man could be attracted to another, but he did know one thing: his two clients had good taste and they were always in good shape. He made a mental note to consider asking one of his gay friends to go shopping with him next time instead of his girlfriend, Angela. She seemed to always be nicely dressed, but FBI agents like her were not known for their men's fashion sense. *Maybe I could find a gay trainer at the gym to help me shed these extra pounds?*

It was the hallowed ground of the federal court at 312 N. Spring Street, an old art deco building which contained some of the smartest men and women on the bench. The interior of the courtroom was all marble and dark wood. Brent and his clients sat on wooden benches that looked more like church pews than seats.

The gallery was full of people; some attorneys, but mostly reporters who were anxiously awaiting a ruling from Judge Beverly Sterling on Brent's motion for summary judgment. Brent knew that the hearing was a long shot. A similar case challenging California's Proposition 8 had already been appealed and was pending before the United

States Supreme Court. But, every case is different and each has its own life. So far, there had been no ruling in Brent's case to stop the locomotive, so he was determined to see it safely into the station.

This was just the type of case that appealed to him: blazing a trail for civil rights; lighting a torch for tolerance. In his early days as a lawyer, he wasn't as fortunate, taking every case that he could just to keep the office doors open. But now, with over 25 years of practice under his slightly bulging belt, he could concentrate on the cases that really meant something: civil rights, consumer rights, governmental abuses... cases that were more than about just paying the bills.

Judge Sterling appeared from her chambers at precisely 9:00 a.m. She demanded promptness from everyone who appeared in her courtroom and applied the same rule to herself. At about 5'4", she looked a little like a child in a Halloween costume or perhaps the judge's daughter, as she strode to the bench in her overflowing black robe. She called the court to order, lowering her voice in an attempt to sound more authoritative, which fell short of its objective due to nasal overtones. She disposed of the entire law and motion calendar, saving Brent's case for last.

"Matter number seven on today's calendar is the case of *Fredericks and Bennett v. County of Santa Barbara.* Counsel, please state your appearances."

Brent rose, traversed the wood-paneled courtroom, and paused in front of the microphone on the counsel table nearest to the jury box. "Brent Marks appearing for the plaintiffs, Your Honor."

Brent's opposition, Ted Penner, forged his way to the opposing counsel's table, cleared his throat, and announced his appearance into the microphone. "Ted Penner for the Intervenor, MarriageProtect.com." Ted had a much too serious look on his face, as if this case were as important to him as it was to Jim and Ron. He believed that marriage was not just a legal relationship, but a holy sacrament ordained by God; and that this sacrament would be tarnished by same-sex marriages. Ted's client had fathered Proposition 8 in California against gay marriage, which had been the ballot initiative with the largest grass roots support in U.S. history. Homophobia was alive and well in America.

Judge Sterling tried to compensate for her lack of powerful voice with a serious look that she launched with a frown as she regarded both counsel with brown pupils over her half-moon glasses, as if she were a drill sergeant looking over a fresh new set of recruits in boot camp.

"I understand that the County of Santa Barbara, the State of California, and the Governor have declined to participate in this action as party defendants."

Brent rose to address the court, as is required in federal court procedure, and took advantage of the open door that had been left for him by Judge Sterling. "That is correct, Your Honor. The State of California believes, as do I, that Proposition 8 is unconstitutional."

"Mr. Marks, I also understand that your request for a writ of mandate to compel the County Clerk of Santa Barbara to issue a marriage license to your clients is based on the case of *Hollingsworth v. Perry,* is that correct?"

"Yes and no, Your Honor."

"That's not exactly an unequivocal answer, Mr. Marks. Which is it? Is it yes or is it no?" *Federal judges would make lousy doctors. Why bother with this medical treatment? You're going to die anyway and we need the bed space.*

"My clients' petition is based on the same principles that the Ninth Circuit was presented with in *Hollingsworth v. Perry,* such as equal protection under the law and due process; but also, under California law as it stands, same-sex couples already have all the rights as opposite sex couples under the law before Proposition 8. It denies my clients their right to designate their relationship as a marriage."

"Isn't that what the Ninth Circuit said in its ruling on the *Hollingsworth* case?"

"Yes, Your Honor."

"Then why should this court not stay these proceedings until the *Hollingsworth* ruling has been considered by the United States Supreme Court?"

"Your Honor, my clients are not the same parties as in *Hollingsworth,* and they are entitled to have their case considered on its merits." *Obviously, she's not buying it. But you never know. Sometimes they ask a question just to throw you off your game.*

"Mr. Penner, how do you weigh in on this?"

Penner stood up anxiously and spoke too quickly. "Your Honor, the issues in this case are identical to those in *Hollingsworth.* If the Court were to rule in favor of the plaintiffs in this case and they were issued a marriage license, and then the Ninth Circuit's ruling in *Hollingsworth* were overturned by the Supreme Court, any ruling this Court would make could potentially be moot.

The Supreme Court has the last say on what is the law of the land. As an Article III court, this Court cannot presume to second guess what it will do."

Sterling's eyebrows lifted. That was exactly what she wanted to hear.

"I agree with Mr. Penner, Mr. Marks. I think it is best to defer ruling on your petition until the Supreme Court makes a decision in the *Hollingsworth* case. A further status conference on this matter will be set by the Clerk, at which time we will take a look at whether the Supreme Court has spoken on the issue."

"Your Honor..." Brent interjected.

"Mr. Marks, is there any urgent reason that your clients need to be married right now as opposed to after the Supreme Court has made its decision?"

"No, Your Honor."

"Then, that will be the order of the Court. Thank you all."

The judge went on to call her next case, and Brent packed up his briefcase and joined his clients as they left the courtroom, dejected. Brent waved off questions being shouted by a crowd of reporters who had congregated in the corridor outside the courtroom. Losers make lousy press conferences.    Penner, however, eagerly jumped into the fray like he was falling off the stage into a mosh pit.

As Brent and his clients trudged away, before he could even have the chance to console them, Joshua Banks, a bible-thumping, homophobic, religious fanatic, blocked their path.  Brent had had run-ins with Banks several times, to the point where he had been forced to obtain a restraining order against him because of death threats.    But he was mainly a zealot and a windbag who was always preaching to anyone who would listen, and a lot of people who wouldn't.

"Marriage should be honored by all, and the marriage bed kept pure!" Banks proclaimed, lifting his finger in front of them as if he was giving a sermon.

"Step aside, Mr. Banks.  Do I have to get another restraining order against you?"

"Men committed acts with other men, and received in themselves due penalty for their perversion!"

"Who is this guy?"

"He's just a nut job, James.  I've dealt with him before."

Banks stepped out of the way and the three proceeded down the escalator to the lobby of the courthouse.

"He's a religious fanatic. Part of the group opposing gay marriage."

As they descended, they could hear the echoes of Banks yelling verses from the Bible.

"These dreamers pollute their own bodies, reject authority and slander celestial beings!"

"He's really harmless. Just ignore him."

"Sounds like he's got a screw loose," said Jim.

Brent nodded. "More than one screw, I think." The bellowing began to fade from their ears as they descended.

"Neither the sexually immoral nor idolaters nor male prostitutes nor homosexual offenders, not thieves, nor the greedy or drunkards nor slanderers nor swindlers will inherit the kingdom of God!"

"I guess it's official, Jim. We're both going to hell."

"At least we'll be there together."

# CHAPTER TWO

Brent bade farewell to his two clients in the underground parking lot of the Los Angeles Mall, across the street from the Spring Street courthouse. He had declined their offer that morning to make the long drive together. It was always better for him to have the solitude of the drive to think before any court hearing.

He took the 5 Freeway to avoid the traffic. Los Angeles had four different rush hours: morning, evening, lunchtime and anytime that wasn't between midnight and four in the morning. Brent attempted to pass around the before-lunchtime traffic, but was held up in a brake light party through the Los Feliz area. As much as he enjoyed arguing a case in federal court, he much preferred to have a state case in good old Santa Barbara.

Less than two hours later, he cracked the window to smell the fresh ocean breeze along the Rincon. *Almost home,* he thought to himself as he glanced out the driver's side window at the crashing waves. He exited the freeway at Coast Village Road so he could enjoy the short drive along the coast.

As a young attorney just starting his practice, he had selected Santa Barbara not because of the fact that he spoke Spanish (which did help him establish his practice because of the large amount of Spanish speaking potential clients who lived there), but because of its "frequency." Santa Barbara felt good for Brent's soul.

It was for the same reason that Ron and Jim had decided to settle there, as well. Santa Barbara, unlike other cities in Southern California, had that home-town feeling. It was still a place where you could still go next door to your neighbor and borrow a stick of butter or cup of sugar. They felt more at ease being in public there and, during the three years they had lived in Santa Barbara, had made friends with more of their neighbors than either of them had made in Los Angeles in the previous ten.

Upon entering the office, Brent's secretary, Melinda, greeted him with a cheery smile and a small handful of messages. Melinda appeared to be the type who could be the subject of dumb blonde jokes; but in her case, none of them would apply.

"Afternoon, boss."

"Hey, Mims. Anything important here?" he asked as he took the messages from her neatly manicured hand, finished with cherry red polish. *How does she type with those?*

"Angela just called. She said if you got back in time, she'd like to meet you for lunch."

"When did she call?"

"About fifteen minutes ago."

Brent stepped into the inner office and tossed his messages onto the walnut desk. *I'll check emails later.* He sat down and dialed Angela.

"Agent Wollard."

"Agent Wollard, I have a very important case for you to solve."

"Oh, yeah?" Angela laughed. "What case is that?"

"The case of the hungry boyfriend."

"This would be my gay rights advocate boyfriend?"

"One in the same – people's rights, actually."

"Yes, I forgot – people's rights. Gays have the same rights as all people."

"Damn right they do."

It was a lovely day, so they decided to meet at the Courthouse Café, which was right across the street from the old courthouse and within walking distance of both Angela's and Brent's offices. For a place through which had trudged such heartbreak and misery – murder, assault, fraud – over its 85-plus years of existence, the garden of the courthouse bloomed with life and beauty like the Garden of Eden.

Lunch with Angela – any time spent with her really – always seemed to pass too quickly, whether there was too much to say and not enough time in which to say it, or just enjoying each other's company without saying a word.

The peace of the moment was broken when Angela glanced at her watch and said, "Wow!"

"What?"

"I'm late, that's what."

"But we just got here."

"Yeah, an hour ago."

"Okay – off you go – I'll get the check. We don't want the Government to lose any of your precious time."

"Don't start on the Government, Brent," she said with a frown.

"I'm not, I'm not." He smiled, assuredly. Brent had a love-hate relationship with the Government. He hated what it had become over the years and loved to make an issue about it.

\*\*\*

When Brent made it back to the office, he didn't even have a chance to go over the messages because Ron and Jim were sitting in the waiting room.

"Hey, guys, I thought we already had our time together," Brent chuckled. He could tell from the serious look on Ron's face that neither one of them was in the joking mood.

"We need to talk."

"Okay, then. Come on in."

Brent ushered them into his office, and planted himself behind the desk as they wiggled into the too-hard wooden client chairs.

21

"What can I help you with?" he asked them.

"We've been attacked," said Jim.

"Attacked? Did you call the police?"

"We just came from there. They won't do anything without a restraining order," said Ron.

Jim and Ron had stopped off for lunch on the way back from court, and by the time they arrived home, they had a surprise waiting for them. Their front window had been shattered by a large rock. But it was no case of ordinary vandalism. The perpetrator had left a message on the voice mail at Jim's office.

"It was that nut, Joshua Banks."

"Can I hear the message?"

Jim played the voice mail for Brent, who immediately recognized the preachy voice of Joshua Banks:

*There is a time to throw stones and a time to gather stones. You shall not lie with a male as one lies with a female! It is an abomination, punishable by death. So sayeth the Lord our God and his will shall be done!*

"I don't know about you, but that sounds like a threat to me," said Ron.

"It certainly does. We'll get a restraining order to keep him away from you. I can prepare the papers today and get a temporary order tomorrow morning. In the meantime, I suggest that you install a good security system."

"We never thought we'd have to deal with something like this in Santa Barbara." Jim put his hand on his forehead in emotional frustration. Ron put his arm around Jim's shoulder to comfort him. "I just hope this piece of paper is enough to protect us."

# CHAPTER THREE

Before putting the finishing touches on his application for a restraining order against Joshua Banks, Brent had the unpleasant task of placing a call to Banks to give him notice that he would be in court the next morning to seek a temporary restraining order. He would have delegated the task to Melinda, but the last time she had a conversation with Banks, it had left her with a strong case of the jitters. Death threats tend to do that sometimes. Brent himself had purchased a handgun for protection after his first run-in with Banks, but later came to believe that Banks' bark was bigger than his bite. Brent punched in his telephone number.

"Mr. Banks? This is attorney Brent Marks."

The other end of the line was quiet. *Maybe he's trying to think of a bible verse to reply with.*

"Mr. Banks? Can you hear me?"

"He who has ears to hear, let him hear."

"Good. Mr. Banks, are you represented by counsel? Do you have a lawyer?"

"Lawyers! They weigh men down with burdens hard to bear, while they themselves will not even touch those burdens with one of their fingers!"

"I take that as a no?"

"You surely can, Counselor. I know why you have summoned me."

"I'm not sure you do. I need to inform you that I will be in Dept. 1 of the Superior Court tomorrow at 8:30 a.m. to seek a restraining order against you for James Frederick and Ronald Bennett."

"Men who lay with other men! An abomination! No one enters suit justly; no one goes to law honestly."

"Just the same, you're invited to be there tomorrow, if you wish to oppose the order."

"You rely on empty pleas, Counselor: you speak lies! You conceive mischief and give birth to iniquity!"

"Good-bye, Mr. Banks." The phone was still vibrating as he set it down.

***

Brent opened to door to his Harbor Hills home and noticed a blurry orange and white streak fly out the door. It was his cat, Calico; a look-alike of the Cheshire cat on Alice in Wonderland – just as cheery, but not as fat. She quickly made a U-turn and reversed direction, running back into the house and making a bee-line for the kitchen. It was dinner time.

Brent set down his laptop, hung up his jacket, and went into the kitchen to lull Calico's wailing into purring and crunching. Then he looked around the room. *Must be a bachelor's house.* Brent wasn't usually a messy housekeeper, but he had just finished a trial and a lot of things were out of place. The living room was not so bad, but the bedroom looked like the dressing room at Saks Fifth Avenue at closing time, with casual clothes draped over the back of the couch and a pile of crumpled suits waiting for the dry cleaners on the cushions.

*Angela's gonna kill me if she sees this.* Brent stuffed the dry cleaning into a bag and put it in the trunk of his car. He folded the casual shirts and put them in the drawer and was just about to straighten the unmade bed when he heard a key turning in the front door.

"Hey, baby, you straightening up your room?"

"How did you know?" Brent laughed and went into the living room and gave Angela a hug.

"It's always a pleasure to see this view. Even with the clothes hanging all over the place, all you can see in your house is the harbor." Angela took off her jacket and hung it on the coat rack.

"I dare you to find one stitch of clothing out of place." Brent turned to admire the view. *She's right. It is spectacular, and it'll get even better towards sunset.*

The afternoon light streamed through the floor to ceiling glass panels as if it were a spotlight on Angela, giving her light brown hair a golden tint and turning her green eyes turquoise. Brent admired the sight. *She's so beautiful.*

Angela was an FBI agent; Brent a lawyer. Neither occupation was a stranger to stress.

Together, they seemed to fit and complement each other, even though they often fought on different "sides." They seemed to be spending almost all of their off time together now. The cat rushed up to Angela and rubbed her leg from whiskers to tail, then reversed direction as it slinked back against her leg.

"Calico, did you miss me?"

"We both did."

Angela sat on the couch and the cat leaped into her lap, rolled around until she found a cozy spot, and turned on her motor.

"So, should we share stories?" Angela caressed Calico and scratched under her chin, causing a louder purr.

"I've got another restraining order against Joshua Banks."

"The religious nut?"

"Yup."

"Who's he offended this time?"

"He threw a rock through Jim Fredericks's and Ron Bennett's window."

"Was anyone hurt?"

"Not this time, but we do need to send him a strong message."

"Of course."

"How's the Federal Bureau of Investigation holding up today?"

"Not a lot of things going on, thankfully."

"No crimes to solve in the megalopolis of Santa Barbara?"

"Doesn't look that way."

"Then our streets are safe for dining tonight?"

"I thought we could stay at home. You have anything? It's my turn to cook."

"We've got some beef."

"Good. I'll make stroganoff."

Angela settled in to prepare the dinner in the kitchen while Brent went off to shower and change out of his street clothes. When he returned, he saw her holding a paper towel to her finger. She had dropped the knife on the counter.

"I cut myself." She frowned in frustration.

Brent held her, and pulled the paper towel away from her finger to examine the wound.

"It's not so bad. But let's wash it and put some antibiotic cream on it. Meat's got a lot of bacteria."

He looked at the knife. A drop of bright red blood was smeared on the blade.

# CHAPTER FOUR

Surprisingly to Brent, Joshua Banks did show up in court; but not with counsel.  After a brief conference with the judge (during which His Honor received a mini-course on how only God can judge your fellow man), miraculously, he agreed to a mutual restraining order.  He would be ordered to stay 50 yards away from Ron and Jim and their property and places of employment, and they would be ordered to stay away from him.  Just as it seemed to be rolling along more smoothly than it should have, the issue of attorney's fees came up.  Banks refused to pay for James and Ron's fees.

"I don't want to have to eat these fees, Brent. We have to make him pay."

"Ron, the thing is: to do that, we have to ask the court to make an order on who is the prevailing party, to force the losing party to pay

33

the fees. There can't be a prevailing party without a specific finding. That means a hearing, which is what we were trying to avoid in the first place."

Judge Michael Perry was obviously disappointed with the news. The expression on his weathered face looked like he had just taken a whiff of rotten eggs. He didn't have time for games. He had a full house and had to move matters along in his courtroom. He decided to forge ahead and finish off this dispute so he could take care of the other numerous cases that were cluttering his calendar.

"What's he doing?"

"He's putting on your trial, Ron. Get ready to testify."

"Madame Clerk, please swear in the parties."

That proved to be a problem in and of itself: not with Ron and James, who each raised their right hand and swore to tell the truth, but with Banks. When asked to stand and take the oath, he exploded.

"I shall not swear an oath at all! Neither by heaven, for it is God's throne!" Banks raised his arm in the air as if he were holding Liberty's torch.

Judge Perry then went into a long-winded explanation of what an affirmation was and advised Banks that he could affirm that he would tell the truth instead of taking an oath.

"Mr. Banks, will you take an affirmation that you are telling the truth?"

Banks looked insulted. With wide eyes, he exclaimed, "God tells us to speak the truth to one another. I always do so."

"I will take that answer as "yes". Is that correct, Mr. Banks?"

"Yes, sir, you most certainly can."

"Good. Mr. Banks, I understand that you wish to represent yourself in this matter, is that correct?"

"Yes, sir, I do."

"Are you absolutely sure about that? Because we are going to hold a hearing on the matter of attorney's fees and you have the right to have counsel for that."

"I am not alone, sir. God stands with me."

"Now, Mr. Banks: in the supporting papers you have been accused of throwing a rock through the Petitioners' window. Technically that is a crime, and you have a Fifth Amendment privilege not to testify against yourself. Do you understand that you don't have to say anything about this and don't have to answer any questions?"

"Yes, sir."

"Good. Then let's proceed. Mr. Marks, please call your first witness."

"I call Ronald Bennett."

Ron testified that when he and Jim arrived home that day, they found their window broken. The apparent weapon was a rock that was sitting among the shards of broken glass on the floor of their living room. Then he testified that they had received the voicemail, and played it for the judge. As the tape played, Banks rocketed out of his seat at counsel table and raised his hand high in the air, like a nerdy guy in sixth grade who's got the answers to all the teacher's questions.

"Whosoever shall conceal his transgressions will not prosper. I must confess that it was I who cast that stone! And I will beg for God's mercy!"

Banks hung his head down in shame.

"Mr. Banks, please sit down. The court will order Mr. Banks to pay the Petitioners' attorney's fees and costs of $1,800."

"Great job, Brent." Ron winked at Brent, who had yet to say a word in the hearing. Brent smiled, packed up his briefcase, and ushered his clients out of the courtroom.

As they walked down the corridor, they could hear Banks' voice echoing after them.

"Marriage is a sacred vow between a man and a woman!"

"Seriously, Brent, that guy needs to get a life." Ron looked back at Banks.

"Don't give him an audience."

"It was the Lord God who made a woman from the rib of the man and brought her to the man! A man shall lay with a woman, not another man!"

Ron motioned with his head toward Banks. "Maybe he should lay with a woman. It might calm him down."

# CHAPTER FIVE

Detective Roland Tomassi from the Santa Barbara Sheriff's Department pulled up to 12600 Foothill Road at the same time as his team of forensic specialists and a compliment of patrolmen that had been sent to deal with the crime scene. Tomassi stepped out of his plain old white Crown Vic in slacks that were just as plain, a shirt that used to be white, and a black tie: standard uniform for homicide detectives. He had seen plenty of murder scenes before, but could not have been prepared for this one. He wiped his sandy brown hair out of his eyes. *Time for a haircut.*

Tomassi instructed two uniformed officers to cordon off the scene and secure it from invasion. Then he briefed the other two uniformed officers to surround the perimeter, look for signs of entry, and await his orders. After a few minutes, they indicated by radio that they were in place and had found no signs of forced entry. Tomassi instructed them to hold their positions while he entered the house.

Tomassi donned booties to prevent contamination, took his shotgun, and instructed Deputy Henley to follow him inside. Upon entering, he saw the bodies, but did not stop to investigate until the entire scene had been secured. The scent of copper, blood and what smelled like a dirty toilet lingered in the air and seemed to soak into his mouth and hair. He continued into the kitchen, where he noticed that blood had been spattered in the sink along with several pieces of blood-soaked paper that had been wadded together. *Probably used it to paint the words on the wall.* He checked the kitchen pantry and under the sinks, being careful not to disturb any latent fingerprints that may have been left on them.

Upon securing the kitchen, Tomassi, leading with his shotgun and followed by Henley, moved down the corridor. There was a long path of blood-stained carpet which led to the end, but Tomassi resisted the urge to follow it right away. Instead, he peered into the bathroom off the hallway and looked behind the shower curtain while Henley stood at watch outside.

Then Tomassi went into the guest bedroom almost directly opposite the bathroom, carefully entering and looking from side to side. He peeked under the bed, which was neatly made, and looked in the closets. *Nobody here.*

They continued their search by following the trail of blood to the master bedroom. It was a slaughterhouse, saturated with that coppery smell. It was almost impossible to tell that the bed sheets had been white, they were so soaked with it. Blood spatters all over the walls, ceiling and closet doors looked like they had been made by a maniac artist throwing red paint from a huge brush. There were several pools of blood on the floor, which led to the red trail they had followed into the bedroom. They checked every possible hiding place in the master bedroom, which appeared clear, and then checked the attic, which had a trap door entrance from the corridor. Finally, when the site appeared to be secured, Tomassi allowed the forensics team to come in.

By that time, the medical examiner had arrived. Tomassi's forensic photographer flashed off numerous pictures of the bodies from every possible angle while the medical examiner from the Coroner's office, Dr. Ignacio Perez, surveyed the scene. It looked unreal – like some macabre photo shoot or a horror movie set.

"This is a messy one," Dr. Perez commented as he slipped on a pair of rubber gloves. The gashes in the knife-pummeled bodies even made Perez's skin crawl.

"Yeah, you never get used to seeing this. Looks like a hate crime. The victim's sister reports they were a gay couple."

"Whatever turns a human being into the animal who did this has got to be more than hate," said Perez as he squatted down to examine the bodies while one of his investigators took body temperatures.

"Animals don't do this," said Tomassi, to the nodding agreement of the doctor.

"Cause of death of both victims appears to be multiple stab wounds. You're most likely looking for a military knife, like a K-Bar. A kitchen knife could never have done all this damage."

"So far, we haven't found any possible murder weapon," said Tomassi, whose team would photograph, sketch, log and bag any item they found that could possibly be used to stab.

Perez took the clipboard from his investigator and examined it.

"I'd say they have been dead for approximately nine hours, but we'll have a better reading back at the morgue."

"That makes it about four in the morning. Henley, take a few men and canvass the entire neighborhood. I want to know where the neighbors were and what, if anything, they saw or heard."

"Yes, sir." Officer Henley turned and left.

"It looks like they were killed in the bedroom, then dragged here and posed."

"Let's have a look." The doctor carefully maneuvered the corridor to the bedroom, followed by Tomassi.

Since the photographer and videographer had finished with the interior and had gone outside to shoot the exterior and the crowd of onlookers, the house was now a mass of activity, with each person carefully doing his or her own job while, at the same time, being aware of the protocol not to contaminate any evidence. Blood samples were taken from each pool of blood and carefully marked. A fingerprint expert examined every surface of the house for latent prints. The victims' finger and foot prints would be taken by the Coroner's Office.

Tomassi and Perez entered the master bedroom, and Tomassi pulled out his pad and began sketching.

"You'll want to get your blood spatter expert in here, but I'd say, from the amount of blood on the sheets and the mattress, that the stabbing began and probably finished on the bed. They definitely were killed here," said Perez.

Perez and his investigator bagged up the bodies and took them out to the coroner's van. That left behind a bloody spot on the living room rug, which had soaked into the wood laminate floor, as well as a series of lingering questions.

# CHAPTER SIX

Detective Rhonda Salas arrived on the death scene about the time Tomassi had developed one huge headache. Homicide detail was never easy, but the gruesome ones always lingered, tormenting his soul. Thankfully, there had not been many of them in Santa Barbara. It had its history of bizarre crimes, but that history could not compare to Los Angeles or even Ventura, its neighbor to the south. Besides the "Mexican" part of the city and the elite areas like Montecito, Santa Barbara was basically a high-middle class village with a lot of retirees and people who enjoyed the life that a quiet little town had to offer.

"What've you got for me, Salas?" Tomassi got right down to business. Detective Salas, even in her conservative dress, was pretty attractive, and Tomassi always had to keep it "strictly business" with her so that his wandering eye would not distract him from his work. But Salas had made it clear with all the guys that not only was she a woman surrounded by men, but she had no interest in them; so they could all forget it. After the jokes had been re-told too many times and discouraged by an audience who, for the most part, had no desire to hear them, Salas had earned respect from her colleagues the usual way one did at the Sheriff's Office: with good police work.

"The couple is Ronald and James Bennett."

"Same last name?"

"They were married last month. James took Ronald's name. His maiden name is Fredericks."

Tomassi's eyebrows raised. He was a little on the macho side and still couldn't get used to the idea of a guy having a maiden name, but it was not an issue at this juncture; just another fact to process.

"But, get this: they had a restraining order against a religious nut who threw a rock in their window and threatened them."

Tomassi suddenly surged with power as his adrenalin switch turned on.

"Have an address?"

"Yes, he lives right here in Santa Barbara."

"Photograph?"

"Yes, here: take the file." Salas handed him the manila folder.

"Good work, Salas. You take over here. I'll take Henley and Davis and their partners and check this guy out."

Tomassi had a short meeting with Henley and Davis and their two partners, then ran to his car, got in, fired it up, and called in to dispatch. Henley and Davis's teams jumped into their patrol cars with the urgency of a brigade of firemen called to a warehouse fire.

\*\*\*

Tomassi parked his Crown Victoria in front of the home of Joshua Banks on De La Guerra Street. The two patrol cars staged themselves in front of the driveway. Tomassi exited with his shotgun, and the four officers, each bearing their own, formed a perimeter around the small house. Tomassi and Henley took positions to the left and right of the front door while Tomassi knocked.

"Sheriff's Department!"

The door creaked open and in the opening stood Joshua Banks, who stood looking into the barrels of two raised and aimed shotguns.

"Joshua Banks?"

Banks dropped to his knees, and put his hands above his head.

"Do you have any weapons, Mr. Banks?"

"I am guilty of the sin, peacemaker, I did it! But I shall be forgiven! Let every person be subject to the governing authorities, for there is no authority except from God!"

The spontaneous confession was almost too good to be true.

"Please don't say anything else, Banks, until I have advised you of your rights." Tomassi kept his gun trained on Banks as Henley moved behind him to cuff him.

Banks shivered with fear. "The wicked flee when no one pursues, but the righteous are bold as a lion!"

Tomassi lifted Banks by the arm. "Is there anyone else at home?"

"I shall fear no evil, as Thou art with me!"

"Answer me! Nobody else is here?"

"Just the Lord God and us, my brothers."

The three other uniformed deputies appeared.

"All clear."

"Good. Henley, check the area for possible weapons."

Tomassi led Banks to his living room couch, sat him down, and pulled out his Miranda card. Even though he knew all the questions by heart, he had to read them, verbatim, from the card or the arrest could be tainted.

Deputy Henley turned his head to look at the area around them. There were stacks of magazines against every wall, which themselves held at least 100 hanging crosses of different assorted sizes and materials. Books, bibles and bible study literature were strewn all over the room. There was no table that did not have at least one statue of Jesus or the Virgin Mary amongst other clutter, and none had any surface exposed. The house smelled like old newspapers (of which there were many stacked in piles around the room) and days-old food.

"Yes, sir. But I think the Health Department would be better suited to deal with this place."

"Or the Fire Department." Deputy Davis began to move a stack of bibles next to them.

"Don't touch those! They are holy! And your hands are unclean!"

Banks wiggled on the couch, bucking against his restraints.

"Holy, holy, is the Lord Almighty; the whole earth is full of his glory!"

Tomassi grabbed Banks by the shoulders and looked into his eyes. "Mr. Banks! Be still and listen to me!"

"Yes, peacemaker, I shall."

"You are under arrest for the murder of…"

Banks' mouth dropped and his eyes opened wide.

"Murder? Who is the unfortunate victim of this heinous sin?"

"Ronald and James Bennett."

"Yea, I did cast the stone, but I did not violate the Seventh Commandment. What citizen accuses me of this vile act, peacemaker? With his mouth the godless man would destroy his neighbor, but by knowledge the righteous are delivered!"

Banks attempted to stand up, but Tomassi gently but forcefully pushed him back down and looked him in the eyes.

"Mr. Banks, you have the right to remain silent. Do you understand that?"

"For Zion's sake, I shall not keep silent! And for Jerusalem's sake, I will not keep quiet until her righteousness goes forth like brightness, and her salvation shines like a torch that is burning."

"What is that gibberish he's saying?" Davis looked uneasy as he checked behind the stacks of rubble.

"They're verses from the Bible." Henley continued to poke around the piles gingerly.

"Now, Mr. Banks, I must continue to read you your rights, and you have to indicate whether you understand. You have the right to remain silent. Do you understand?"

"A fool hath no faith in understanding, but that his heart may discover itself."

"You have to answer *yes* or *no*. Do you understand that you have the right to remain silent?"

"Yes, peacemaker. Even a fool who keeps silent is considered wise."

Undeterred, Tomassi kept reading from his Miranda card.

"Anything you say may be used against you in court. Do you understand?"

"Yes, but there is only one lawgiver; and that is the Lord our God. Who is man to judge his neighbor?"

"Please, just say yes or no. You have the right to the presence of an attorney before and during any questioning. Do you understand?"

"Yes. I would like to call my pastor."

"You can talk to the jailer about that. Now let me finish, please. You have the right to the presence of an attorney before and during any questioning. Do you understand?"

"Yes, peacemaker."

"If you cannot afford an attorney, one will be appointed for you, free of charge, before any questioning, if you want. Do you understand?"

"Yes. The Lord sends poverty and wealth. He humbles and He exalts."

"Do you want to talk about what happened?"

Banks looked at the ceiling as if he expected a divine revelation, then stared at Tomassi with blank brown eyes.

"Confess your sins to one another and pray for one another that you may be healed. I will confess only to God, peacemaker; but I do not deny that I cast that stone."

"Are you now denying your involvement in the murder?"

"Yes, sir, I surely do. My enemies speak evil against me!"

"Davis, come with me. I'll drop you off to book His Holiness. Henley, stay here and secure the property until we get the search warrant. Nobody goes in, understood?"

"Yes, sir."

Tomassi and Davis marched off with Banks between them: two Roman soldiers escorting the accused to the den of lions.

# CHAPTER SEVEN

Dr. Perez frowned in frustration as he counted, for the second time, the gashes on the body of James Fredericks Bennett. *Twenty six!* Multiple stab wounds to the chest and back and five of them had penetrated vital organs – any one of which could have caused his death. Ron Bennett's body had twenty one gashes. He heard a buzz at the door and looked up to see Roland Tomassi.

"Hello, Roland. My report's not done yet."

"I know, Doc. I just came to see if there was anything you could tell me at all."

"Both victims had multiple stab wounds to the chest and back, penetrating the heart, lungs and liver. Any of those could have been the cause of death. And James Bennett also had wounds to the stomach and intestines."

"How many stab wounds?"

"Twenty one on Ronald and twenty-six on James."

"Yikes."

"Like I thought, you're looking for a military-style knife (probably a K-Bar), about seven inches long. I figure the perpetrator or perpetrators first attacked both victims with precision strikes to the vitals. Any one of the first five strikes would have disabled them and caused death. He's probably done this before: may be military or ex-military."

"Why so many other stab wounds if any of the first five did the trick?"

"He, or *they,* were just having fun."

*\*\*\**

Rhonda Salas looked up from the Bennett file, which was spread all over her desk. She had to take a break from the carnage. Eight hundred digital photographs had been taken, and she had selected 100 of them to print. *What kind of monster can do something like this?* She felt relief, for the first time, that she herself didn't have a partner.

They had not released key details of the murders to the press, such as the type of murder weapon, and they had not made an issue out of the fact that the victims were gay; but the media, of course, used that as its teaser. After all, the victims had already made the news as Santa Barbara's latest same-sex newlywed couple.

As she flipped through all the evidence and the photographs of the search of Joshua Banks' home, Rhonda thought about how simply a murder case is portrayed by the media: just the assembly of pieces of a puzzle until it was all figured out. But in real police work it was never that simple.

She thought of the only suspect that they had in custody. He seemed to be so obvious, and he was a nut. But he just didn't seem to fit the profile, and she had thought Tomassi was jumping the gun to arrest him right away. Banks was a hoarder with no military background, and nothing was found in the search of his home: nothing except books, newspapers, magazines, and bible memorabilia. But no knives. It was such a mess that the search team didn't even know where to begin. Tomassi slipped in at the desk opposite her.

"Solve the case yet, Salas?"

"Well, for one thing, I don't think it's our guy."

"I know what you mean. He's a nut case, for sure, but he looked genuinely surprised when I told him they had been murdered."

Tomassi related the information to her that he had learned from Dr. Perez and she filled him in on the search results (which were, essentially, no results).

"Looks like we're pretty much back where we started." Rhonda ran her fingers through her dark brown hair and leaned her elbow on the desk.

"Has our bible-thumper chosen a lawyer yet?"

"No. I think he's going to end up with the public defender."

"Well, let's go talk to him, then."

\*\*\*

The Deputy brought Banks to the interrogation room and cuffed his ankle to the table. Tomassi and Salas watched him for a couple of minutes through the two-way mirror. Banks was looking up at the ceiling and babbling, clasping his handcuffed hands together and shaking them in the air.

"What's he doing?" Salas strained to look through the mirror.

"Praying. You would, too, if you were in that chair."

Salas and Tomassi opened the door and sat down across from Banks.

"Mr. Banks, you remember me, don't you?"

"Yes, peacemaker. The memory of the righteous is a blessing, but the name of the wicked will rot."

"This is my associate, Detective Salas. We'd like to talk to you."

"Yea, I will speak; but not without my counselor."

"You have a lawyer?"

"He will plead my soul's cause. He will redeem my life."

"Who is he?"

"His Christian name is Brent Marquez. But I believe he goes by the name of Marks now."

"Brent Marks?" Salas looked surprised. "He was the victims' lawyer."

"And he shall be mine as well. It is the will of God."

"Salas, call Marks.  Tell him God's got a job for him."

# CHAPTER EIGHT

When Brent received the call from the Sheriff's Office, he was shocked. Of course, it was not the weirdest thing that had ever happened to him in his practice. *This one should be easy. The victims were my clients. Banks is the accused perp. Even though he probably didn't do it, I should declare a conflict.*

Brent wrestled with the idea on the way to the jail. As a lawyer, he often found himself at the crossroads where morality, ethics, and duty collided. He was the ultimate arbiter of these inner conflicts. The authorities would sort it out later if he had made a mistake. *I'm supposed to be done with criminal cases, anyway. But Banks? A murderer? That doesn't fit.*

The potential case nagged at Brent. As he sat in his car in the parking lot, he decided to call the State Bar ethics hotline. This was a time when he would have called Charles Stinson, his mentor; but there was no hotline to heaven, unless Banks had already hooked into it. *Must be a party line.*

"State Bar hotline, may I help you?"

Brent explained the quandary he was in.

"Technically, the attorney-client privilege survives after death, but only so long as the estate of the decedent's estate is represented."

"So I would need the consent of the estate's representative?"

"If your representation involved any possible client communications, yes. Also, the appearance of impropriety is something you should look at. If it looks improper, it probably is."

Brent disconnected. He felt no better off after the call than he did before it. He exited the car and headed into the jail. It was a creepy place to be, even for someone who had the freedom to leave whenever he chose. Confining noises reverberated throughout the concrete and metal – it was not the nicest place in the County of Santa Barbara.

Banks was sitting on the inmate side of the attorney conference room in a blue jail jumpsuit. To Brent, he looked smaller than he usually did.

Maybe that was because he had to keep quiet in here.

"Hello, Mr. Banks."  Brent took a seat opposite him."

"Counselor!  Praise God you have come!"

"Now, Mr. Banks, please don't tell me anything about your case.  I've decided I can't even consider taking it unless the estate of my clients consents."

"Wicked and deceitful mouths have been opened against me, speaking guile with evil tongues!"

"Say no more, Mr. Banks.  I can't discuss it with you.  But if you sign this consent, I'll ask Mr. Bennett's sister to sign it and, if she does, I can come back here and then we can talk about your case."

"God has sent you to me.  Why should I sign a paper?"

Brent stood up.  "This conversation is over, Mr. Banks.  I can recommend a good lawyer to you."

"Wait! Wait!"

Brent turned to see Banks holding up his cuffed hands, as if he was reaching for something.

"By God, I will sign."

Brent sat back down, withdrew a pen, showed it and the paper to the Deputy on call, who nodded and then gave the pen and paper to Banks. Banks signed and handed the paper and pen back to Brent.

"If Susan Fredericks consents, I'll be back to see you again."

"I shall see you again, Counselor, if it is God's will."

\*\*\*

"That's what you called me in here for?" Susan Fredericks stood up from her chair, enraged.

"Susan, calm down. I wouldn't have asked you if I thought he did it."

"What makes you think he didn't do it?"

"If you just sit down, I'll tell you."

Susan eased back down in her seat. "I'm listening."

Brent spoke mostly with his hands. Hunches are not easy to put into words.

"Think about it. He's the most obvious suspect. He threw the rock, and admitted that in court. But, when the cops questioned him, he seemed surprised to hear about the murders."

"So, he's a good actor."

"That's just it. He's not a good actor. Remember how he blurted out in court that he threw the rock, and asked for God to forgive him?"

"Yes."

"I just have a feeling about this one, Susan. And I don't think I even need your consent. I just would feel better if I had it."

Susan looked Brent straight in the eyes, like a stare-out.

"I have one condition."

"What is that?"

"You have to find out who did it."

Brent's eyes stayed locked on Susan's while she tightened her lips during the challenge.

"That may be Banks' only defense."

# CHAPTER NINE

Judge Burt Hendron was always friendly. Most of the lawyers who appeared before him called him "Uncle Burt." Not to his face, of course; but he knew about the nickname and it didn't seem to bother him. He had a monotone mumble and started almost every sentence with "Well now" and finished them with "Okay, fine." Lawyers in the courthouse used to joke that, in handing down a death sentence, he would probably say, *"Well now, you're remanded to the custody of the California State Department of Corrections where you will be put to death, okay? Fine."* Hendron took the bench and looked around the courtroom at the dregs of society that composed his arraignment court. Families of loved ones gone astray, seeking their freedom (and bail money back), assorted lawyers (including members of the public defender's office), the deputy district attorneys with their shopping carts full of files, bail bondsmen, and, of course, the stars of the show: the ones who stood accused of various felonies and misdemeanors. Uncle Burt's round face, mixing-bowl cut bangs of graying blond locks, and toothless smile made him look more like an emoticon than a judge.

"Well now, we're going to call the case of People of the state of California versus Joshua Banks. Okay? Fine. Counsel, please state your appearances."

"Brent Marks for the defendant, Your Honor."

"Leslie Ford for the People, Your Honor."

"Well now, Mr. Marks. Your client is charged with first degree double murder."

"Yes, Your Honor. My client waives reading of rights and the complaint." Brent motioned to Banks, who sat among the custodies in the jury box, and he stood up.

"Okay, fine. To the charge of murder in the first degree of Ronald Bennett and James Bennett, Mr. Banks, how do you plead?"

"Not guilty, Your Honor." Banks recited the phrase he was instructed, and nothing more.

68

"Okay, fine. Would you like to be heard on the matter of bail?"

"Yes, Your Honor. My client is the Assistant Pastor of Our Lady of Holiness Church in Santa Barbara. He has been a member of the community all his life and has no criminal record. The defendant has property in Santa Barbara and can afford bail to guarantee his appearance."

"Okay, fine. Ms. Ford?"

Ford popped out of her seat like she had just hit the eject button on an F-16, and argued with the same emotion as if it were her brother who had been murdered and not Susan's. *Why are they so emotional?*

"Your Honor, this is a capital case; not to mention a heinous double murder. It would be outrageous to grant bail in this case. The victims in this case were stabbed multiple times in an obvious hate crime! The People will be asking for the death penalty."

"Your Honor, there hasn't been a person put to death in California for years. The constitutionality of the death penalty has been in question for quite some time, and the People are jumping the gun. I doubt this case will survive a preliminary hearing, if that."

"Well, now, Mr. Marks; Ms. Ford is correct that this is a capital crime, and I'm afraid I cannot grant bail, okay? Fine. The defendant is remanded to the custody of the Sheriff. Waive time for preliminary hearing?"

"No, Your Honor."

"Okay, fine. The preliminary hearing is set for May 26th at 8:30 a.m. in Department 6."

Banks was led out by the Bailiff to a holding cell. He would be transferred back to the jail with all the other inmates in custody at the end of the court day.

\*\*\*

At 6:00 p.m., the black and white Sheriff's Department bus was loaded with prisoners for the boring ride back to the Santa Barbara County Jail. The bus was driven by one deputy, and two more sat in the interior to guard the prisoners. As it chugged down Calle Real, the deputies exchanged stories and jokes. Suddenly, a huge truck crashed into the side of the bus, pushed it off the road and toppled it over in an enormous cloud of dust.

*  *  *

Roland Tomassi answered the call. *Why do they need me at a traffic accident?*

"Dispatch – Tomassi. What's this about?"

"See the Deputy on call. Multiple homicides have been reported at the scene."

When Tomassi arrived, he saw the overturned bus surrounded by six Sheriff's patrol cars, blinking lights like Santa Claus Lane on Christmas Eve. He approached the Deputy who appeared to be in charge and showed him his badge.

"You're first on the scene?"

"Yes, sir. Deputy Bruce Johns."

"Any survivors?"

The Deputy shook his head. "All dead."

"Do you have a list of prisoners?"

"No."

"Well get one, man!"

Inside the bus, it looked more like an abattoir than a bus accident. The three deputies' throats had been cut, as well as all the prisoners.

Rhonda Salas pulled up and ran out to the bus to Tomassi.

"Salas, I asked Deputy Johns there for a list of everyone who was on this bus. We're going to need photos, too; especially if someone's missing."

"I'm on it." She ran back to her unmarked car.

Tomassi radioed in for his crime scene crew and barked out orders to the deputies.

"Get this scene sealed off. And get someone to close the road on both sides!"

When the list and photographs finally came in, Tomassi took the gruesome task of matching each body to the photo. The list had ten names on it. The bus held only twelve bodies, including the three deputies.

Tomassi exited the bus covered in dust, his face pale white.

"Salas, put out an APB on Joshua Banks."

# CHAPTER TEN

"Brent, Joshua Banks is on two."

"Tell him to hold."

Melinda appeared in the doorway to Brent's office. *What, a blonde emergency?*

"I think you'd better take this. He's speaking in tongues or something."

"I've gotta go, I'll call you right back." Brent pushed line two. There was a static on the line, and he could hear someone sobbing.

"Mr. Banks?"

*"Kara kak kan ko lo sin. Nara kara poa se. Eh le te la kon ko na tan fee* ! Satan!" *Ro hossh ke la ne ke de de na le. "*

"Mr. Banks?"

"Yea, it is I. I have seen that ancient serpent, the Devil, Satan! Yea, Azazel, Abaddon! And he came to me in the form of an angel!"

"What are you talking about? Where are you?"

*"Am di biddi bittle no ko rama si ka na pu te."*

"Mr. Banks, I can't help you if you don't tell me what's going on. Are you in the jail?"

*"Nea sa bo dinda budu tash ne kal marka.* I am trapped, captured by the evil one who hath brushed me with the powers of darkness! I must pray now, for God to show me the light."

Brent heard dial tone as the phone went dead.

"Detective Tomassi on one!"

Brent picked up the phone.

"Marks, where's your client?"

"I don't know. He just called me."

"Where is he?"

"What's going on?"

74

"He just killed a busload of prisoners and three of my deputies!"

*** 

A pack of sheriffs and Santa Barbara police department black and whites screamed up to the De la Guerra residence of Joshua Banks with lights blazing. The gray Santa Barbara SWAT van stopped in the middle of the street, blocking it, and out of the truck jumped eighteen men in paramilitary uniforms, heavily armed. Tomassi and Salas exited their cars and approached the Sergeant in charge.

"Sergeant: Detectives Tomassi and Salas."

"This your case, Tomassi?"

"Yes."

"Okay. Stand by. If your guy is in there, we'll deliver him."

"Alive, I hope."

"Of course alive, unless he shoots at us first."

Ten members of the team formed a perimeter around the house, while one manned the battering ram at the porch, surrounded by five others. As the officer rammed the door, the one behind him called out "Police!" The door down, they stormed the house like soldiers on a mission.

After a few minutes, Tomassi heard the "all-clear" signal. Nobody was inside.

"Sergeant, I need to take over here."

"Go ahead, Tomassi. It's all yours."

Tomassi and Salas entered with several sheriff's deputies.

Tomassi was squatting on his feet, looking around and under the clutter, when he looked up to see a woman.

"Davis! I thought I told you to seal off the area."

"Detective, I'm Special Agent Wollard of the FBI. I'm here to assist you in your investigation."

Tomassi rose and shook her hand.

"Already you're calling this a serial killing?"

"We've seen the bus."

Tomassi shook his head. *Now I've got the feds up my ass.*

"Alright. I'm waiting for my forensics team."

"They've got to be busy. We can get you a team from Los Angeles."

Tomassi was tempted. The FBI had the most sophisticated crime laboratory in the country.

"That's okay, Wollard. My guys can handle it."

"We're just trying to help."

***

Brent's head was spinning. He was trying to take in all the information and process it, but it was coming in too fast, too hot.

"Brent, there are two sheriff's deputies here to see you."

"Show them in."

The two uniformed deputies, both average height, one brunette and one redhead with freckles, stepped inside Brent's office and stood there, as if at attention.

"Have a seat, gentlemen."

"Thank you." The freckled one pulled out a notebook. "I'm Deputy Salinger and this is Deputy Bingham. We've been sent by Detective Tomassi to take a report."

Brent looked Salinger in the eye. "On what?"

"Your contact with Joshua Banks."

"Mr. Banks is my client. My conversation with him is absolutely privileged."

"Just the same, Detective Tomassi would like to put a trace on your phone, in case he calls in again."

"Sorry, gentlemen, I cannot oblige. Communications with my client, including his location, are privileged."

"Detective Tomassi's not going to like this."

"Deputy Bingham, is it? I have a lot of respect for Detective Tomassi, but I simply cannot agree to this request."

\*\*\*

Toward the end of his day, Brent was feeling low. His client, whom he had thought was not guilty, had apparently committed a mass murder to escape from custody and the police thought that Brent was covering for him. *But what about the truck? He had to have an accomplice.* Brent needed to put the worries of the office out of his mind. He needed home. Naturally, whenever he thought of home, he thought of Angela, so he called her immediately.

"Hey baby."

"Hey." Her voice was cold and mechanical.

"What's wrong?"

"Nothing." Then silence at the other end.

"You still there?"

"Yes. What do you want, Brent?"

*Brent, not honey, not sweetheart. And 'what do you want?' I'm in deep shit, apparently.*

"I had a hard day today. Just thought it would be nice to see you."

"So, whenever you have a bad day, you want me to come over to cheer you up?"

"Something like that."

"Well, I can't come over tonight. I'm busy."

"With what?"

"I'm assisting with the Bennett case, which is more than I can say for you."

*There it is! Attorney/client double whammy.*

"You know he's my client and I can't violate privilege."

"I know all about privilege, Brent, but there has to be a limit to it. We need to find this maniac before he kills again."

"We?"

"We're forming a task force."

"Look, I promise if I hear from him, I'll encourage him to turn himself in."

"That's not good enough."

"What do you want me to do, Angela? Violate my oath? I certainly wouldn't ask you to do that."

"Oh, no?"

"No."

Then she hung up. Brent redialed, but she refused to answer. He left a message.

"Angela, I'm sorry, but this isn't personal. I'll call the Bar hotline when they open tomorrow and see what they say, okay? Please, talk to me."

Brent decided to give her some time to cool off. He headed home to a dark house. Just him and the cat.

# CHAPTER ELEVEN

Angela still hadn't called by the end of the evening, and Brent spent the rest of it sulking, depressed. Calico moved from one favorite spot to another, indifferent to his suffering. Finally, after he had gotten ready for bed, the phone rang.

"Hey, baby."

"The Spirit of Truth has come and will guide you to all truths."

"Mr. Banks?"

Brent quickly hit the 'record' button on his telephone.

There was a pause, and then: "*Oh ka wee no tal banshee deswin.* An angel hath been revealed to me and he shall show thee the way."

A chill ran down Brent's spine.

"Mr. Banks, where are you? You have to turn yourself in. It's the only way. The longer you run, the worse it will be for you."

"It is the glory of God to conceal things, but the glory of kings to search things out. The truth will be revealed; everything in its own time. *In do shin maka nay kot guy das vindat.* It shall be written in blood."

The line went dead. *There was something different about his voice. Something...cold.*

Brent couldn't sleep that night. He was haunted by nightmares. The grisly images from the Bennett case flashed through his mind. In his dreams, he was pursued by a man with a knife. Every time he tried to hide, the man would slash into his hiding place with the knife, like *The Shining.* Finally, after what seemed to be the entire night, he went to sleep.

Brent screamed, and sat up in bed. He was sweating. It was still dark, so he lay in bed and tried to go back to sleep. It was impossible. As dawn broke above the hills, Brent gave up trying to sleep and got up. It was a new day, and that should have held promise of good things, but Brent was still down. And, on top of that, he was fatigued.

At the office, Brent called the State Bar Ethics Hotline. Brent learned that he had the duty to reveal anything that Banks told him if he was in the process of committing a crime or covering one up. That certainly applied to last night's communication.

Angela called him before he had a chance to call and tell her. "Brent, I need you to come here right away."

"Okay, I'll be right over."

"Not at the office. Another crime scene. Banks did it again."

Brent didn't understand why he would be summoned to a crime scene until he got there. It was the home of another gay couple who had recently been married. Brent was stopped at the yellow tape by a sheriff's deputy.

"Let him in." Angela lifted the tape for Brent to slip under.

"I have to warn you, this is not a pretty sight."

The first thing Brent saw when he entered the house was the red writing on the wall:

*Marks – truth is revealed.*

Brent immediately felt faint. The room was spinning. *The truth will be revealed. It shall be written in blood.*

Tomassi glared at Brent with clenched teeth, like he wanted to punch his lights out.

"You wanna explain to me why this lunatic writes your name in blood on the wall?"

"That's what he said last night. 'The truth will be revealed.' And he said it shall be written in blood. But it didn't sound like Banks."

"You talked to him last night?" Angela was angry again.

"I got a phone call at home. I was going to tell you, but…"

"That's it, Marks. No more withholding evidence. I'll have you for obstructing justice!"

"No, you won't. I'll cooperate fully. He's crossed the line and he's outside the privilege now. But I still don't think this guy is Banks."

"Of course it's Banks."

"I'm not so sure, Angie."

"Keep your opinion to yourself. But you have to tell me everything he said. I want every goddamn word."

Brent looked past Tomassi and into the room. There were photographers taking pictures and he recognized Dr. Perez, the Coroner. When they moved, Brent saw two bloody bodies, this time one piled on top of the other, as if in a sexual position. He gagged and turned his head.

"I need to get out of here. Can we talk outside?"

Tomassi nodded and went back to work. Angela led Brent outside. He had turned pale white and was retching.

"Put your hands on your knees. Get some blood to the brain."

*Finally, the maternal instinct kicks in.*

"Angie, I'm...I'm sorry."

"Shh, shh. It's okay." She patted his back gently, then led him to her car and opened the door. "You sit down here in my car and I'll send Tomassi out to talk to you in a few minutes."

Brent sat down and looked up at her. The look in her eyes was warm and comforting. Brent smiled weakly.

Inside the house, Tomassi was consulting with Dr. Perez.

"Death appears to be from multiple stab wounds. Same type of knife as the Bennett murders – six to seven inch blade. Time of death: about seven hours ago."

"Thanks, Doc.  Salas, get us a printout of all marriage licenses issued to same sex couples in the County of Santa Barbara."

"Got it."

"I'll ask for a task force to be set up and get some experts working on profiles for you."

"Thanks, Wollard.  I'm asking for help now."

"I know.  We'll get this guy."

"I'm gonna go talk to Marks."

"Okay.  Don't be too hard on him."

Tomassi flashed a tired half smile and patted Angela on the shoulder as he left the room.

# CHAPTER TWELVE

A task force was formed, with the Santa Barbara Sheriff designated as the lead agency, Roland Tomassi as the lead investigator and Angela Wollard as co-investigator. The FBI contributed its full assistance, including behavioral analysis and research, equipment, funding and manpower.

It was all arranged. Brent would cooperate, but the calls that came to his office would be handled by him and him alone, due to potential confidentiality issues with regard to other clients. The police would have free reign over calls to his home telephone number. For some reason, Banks (or whomever the caller was) had decided to place the calls to him there. On his office calls, he would record any that he received and turn over tapes of any calls from Banks. The telephone company had placed a tap on his phone so that the source of the calls could be identified.

At home, it was no longer just Brent, Calico and the more than occasional visit from Angela. It was Brent, Calico, sometimes Angela, and a full-time Deputy: Salinger, the redhead. He was a lanky, average-looking guy who hadn't seen his first high school reunion yet. But he was quiet, kept to himself, and the cat liked him. Tonight she was the only female present at the Harbor Hills hillside. Angela was pulling the night shift on what the news was already calling "The Honeymoon Stalker" case.

Brent received another late night phone call at about 3 a.m., but this time he was prepared. Every call was traced and automatically recorded.

"Hello?"

"The truth hath been revealed, but thou art not free. You have not learned the lesson."

"Mr. Banks, where are you?"

"I am outside your dimensions. *Ot ki sili naka pheno shtati. Uoth thewonk ton ohw i ma tub i liw leever flesym ot eeth.*"

Once again the phone went dead to dial tone.

"I've got it!" Hanson proudly called his treasure into Tomassi.

Brent was not satisfied with turning over the entire investigation to the police, even if Angela's task force was providing extra investigative muscle. He called his friend and investigator Jack Ruder for a consultation of his own. They met, as they usually did, at a local bar. This time it was The Press Room, a small pub where the beer was cold and the place was quiet. Except for the two guys playing darts in the corner of the bar, the place was almost deserted. Brent slid up to Jack at his table.

Jack had transferred from the LAPD to the FBI, where he had served on several serial killer task forces. A career agent, now retired, he was uniquely qualified to lead this investigation, let alone assist. Brent was shocked because Jack was out of uniform. He was in a blue sweatshirt and jeans, but looked stiff and out of place. Having a mug of beer in his hand didn't do his disguise any justice. Jack looked like a cop who was undercover at a bar to expose a drug deal. In fact, Jack always looked like a cop. He couldn't go undercover, even if everyone was dressed in Halloween costumes.

"Jack, what's up? Are your suits all at the dry cleaner?"

Jack stood up and flashed a goofy smile. It looked goofy probably not because of the smile itself, but the silly wardrobe.

"Well, you told me to be more casual. Et, voila!" Jack turned around to show his outfit.

"What do you think?"

"I think you need a girlfriend. She'd be able to dress you better."

Jack frowned, then sat down. Brent ordered a beer and played the tape for him of both phone calls.

"We need to have these tapes analyzed. The FBI's probably already doing it."

"I'm launching my own investigation, Jack. If this guy is Banks, he can get another lawyer to walk him into the execution chamber. If it's not Banks, I owe it to him to stick on the case."

"You mean solving the murders?"

"That's the only way to defend him, as I see it."

"What makes you think he's not the guy?"

"Alright: Banks is weird - crazy, even. He quotes the Bible and speaks in tongues, but the person who made these phone calls is truly evil. I can feel it."

"Maybe Banks just graduated. Remember when he threatened your life?"

"Yeah, but he's more of an actor than a maniac."

"Sometimes the maniac can be sitting right next to you and you'd never know it."

"When I was just starting out, Charles Stinson got me on the private counsel list to defend alleged parole violators."

"Alleged, humph." Jack took a swig of his beer.

"Exactly. But I remember looking into their eyes. They say that eyes are the windows to the soul. But when I looked into their eyes, I saw emptiness. True evil. Gave me the creeps."

"I know what you mean. But you can't defend Banks by telling a jury to look into his eyes."

"We're going to need a language expert."

***

For the language expert, Brent called on Dr. Jean Beverly. She had assisted him before on another case involving a complicated form of alternative communication. Dr. Beverly was a criminologist and forensic linguist and psychologist, with a PhD in Psychology and Criminology, an M.A. in linguistics, and a B.A. in English with a concentration in linguistics. Brent had Melinda set up an appointment for her to meet with him and Jack in Brent's office to see if she could help.

Dr. Beverly was probably very attractive in her day, which was sometime in the 80s, and she was dressed for the 90s. She packed just a few more pounds than the average woman her age, but she had a pleasant appearance and spoke in an authoritative tone.

"Dr. Beverly, it's great to see you. Come in, please." Jack and Brent both stood up to greet her.

"This is Jack Ruder, our investigator."

"Pleased to meet you, Mr. Ruder."

Dr. Beverly took a seat in one of the wooden chairs opposite Brent's walnut desk. Brent summarized the situation and played the tape of the phone calls for her.

"Some followers of Christ believe that the Holy Spirit can speak through them. That's called speaking in tongues. It certainly sounds like that's what he's doing on the first call you recorded, but on the second, I'm not so sure. Could you play it back for me please?"

*Ot ki sili naka pheno shtati. Uoth thewonk ton ohw i ma tub i liw*

"Stop! Back it up, please."

*Uoth thewonk ton ohw i ma tub i liw leever flesym ot eeht.*

"That is English."

"English?"

"Yes. May I?"

Dr. Beverly pulled the tape player closer to her and played each phrase separately.

"*Uoth thewonk* – Thou knoweth. *Ton ohw I ma* – Thou knoweth not who I am. *Tub i liw leever flesym ot eeht* – But I will reveal myself to thee. He's saying it word for word, but backwards."

"Amazing."

"Actually, it's pretty simple. And the Bible quotations from the first message are from the Bible, alright; but the second one – 'I am outside your dimensions' – that sounds like something from the Satanic Bible."

"The Satanic Bible?"

"Yes, it's a philosophical treatise on Satanism written by Anton LaVey in the 60s. But a lot of Satanic followers treat it as their own scripture."

"Why would a religious fanatic be reading something like the Satanic Bible?"

"Maybe he studied Satanism. You don't have to be a Satanist to study it. Perhaps he read it somewhere and it stuck in his memory as a quote from the Bible."

"Seems to me that this guy is more of a Satanist than a religious zealot."

"The Church of Satan condones same-sex marriages. Christian churches don't. From the profile you supplied me, it is obvious that he is punishing people in same-sex marriages. He's obviously a sociopath or psychopath, who has religious compulsions."

"He seems like a demon to me."

"Whatever he is, what you really need is an expert on religion to help us complete his profile if we are ever to hope to catch him."

"Or an exorcist."

# CHAPTER THIRTEEN

Angela dragged her tired body through the front door of her apartment. It was already close to midnight, and she was too fatigued to be hungry. That is, until her senses registered that something was cooking in her kitchen. She kicked off her shoes in the foyer, hung her jacket on the coat rack, and went to investigate.

"Welcome home from the war."

"Thanks. We're going to eat this late?"

"Just something light. Maine lobster."

Angela harrumphed. "Sounds very light."

"You prefer to save it for lunch tomorrow? It'll make a great salad."

"With this task force duty, lunch is more likely to be burgers. No, let's have it now. It's a great idea."

Angela slumped down in a chair at the kitchen table.

"If I have the energy to eat it."

"Any breaks on the case?"

"No.   We met with the psychologists, linguists and bible experts today.   They're working together on a profile."

"I met with an expert today, too – Jean Beverly."

"Beverly – I know her.  She's good.  You're doing your own investigation?"

"With an altogether different perspective. But I'll share, of course.  Dr. Beverly deciphered some of the tongues on the recording."

"Really?"

"Yeah.  It's English – backwards.  And she said that one of the bible verses came from the Satanic Bible."

"Sounds like we could use her on the team."

"She's made a report for us.  Jack sent it to you by email."

***

He awoke from the dream and remembered every detail of it. *For God speaks in one way, and in two, though man does not perceive it. In a dream, in a vision of the night, when deep sleep falls on men, while they slumber in their beds.*

He knew that he had to do as he had been commanded in the dream. But was not the act of execution the act of killing, and wasn't that a sin? He was confused; but, at the same time, exhilarated that he had been chosen to accomplish this important task. But why did it give him pleasure to hear the cries of the infidels as he slew them? Why did their screams of death give him such pleasure? Why was such emotion attached to this sacred act? Just thinking about it was making him hard. He followed through, giving himself pleasure and experiencing the relief. Then he felt disgusted with himself, that he could do such a despicable act, and prayed for forgiveness.

As he knelt in prayer, he could smell himself. He stunk like a pig – a filthy animal. He had to be clean, to be pure. He rose, went into the bathroom, stepped into the shower, turned on the water as hot as he could stand it, and scrubbed every drop of earthly sweat from his body until he felt that his skin should be raw. Then he dried his body, knelt again, and prayed.

As he prayed, he held the sword of God in front of him and made the sign of the cross with the blade. He balanced the knife on his two hands, left index finger on the blade and right one on the handle, and lifted it to the heavens. He prayed that it shall be blessed and that he shall carry out God's holy mission. He prayed that he would have the strength to carry out his duties in the name of the Lord – that he may avenge God and punish the infidels.

*\*\*\**

The car was piled with empty McDonalds bags and used Styrofoam coffee cups. It smelled like a trash can. He crouched down in the passenger's seat, waiting. Waiting and babbling.

He was in there. The beast – the abomination. But his time was coming near – the time to pay for his sins and be delivered to Hell.

*"Thou shalt bring forth that wicked man or woman, which have committed that wicked thing – and shalt stone them with stones until they die."*

He would draw the sword of the Lord God, and march forthright, without fear, into the temple of the infidels, and slay and execute him for his sins against the Father. And after he did this righteous act, he would be covered in his blood, and let himself be overcome by the Spirit, clearing his mind to allow the message to come through. And, through him, the Spirit would write the message on the wall.

# CHAPTER FOURTEEN

Father Thaddeus Brown was a Franciscan monk who had served the Lord for over 50 years in missions all around the world. He was a stout man, with a body more fit than you would expect from his 73 years, and had a full head of graying hair. During his missions, he had lived in the birthplaces of civilization – Judaism, Islam and Christianity. Not only did he hold doctorate degrees in theology and psychology, but he had also studied each of the similar world religions and their practices.

Father Brown had faith, but he was also a theologian; and that application of divine science to life's reality had caused him to question his faith several times throughout his career.

During his service in Afghanistan, he had been called upon to perform an exorcism on a teenage boy whose family believed him to be possessed by demons. All his professional training could not have prepared him for this experience, and he had to leave the service of the Lord and meditate deeply for two years afterward.

The memories came creeping back to him after one of his former students, Jean Beverly, called him to ask if he would consult on a serial murder case. Whether it was an evil that was created by man, or some divine evil that emanated from a fallen angel, Father Brown was about to look into the eyes of a demon one more time.

Jean had arranged to meet him for tea at the Santa Barbara Biltmore Hotel. The terrace of the Bella Vista was a special place for Brent and Angela, whom Brent had invited to join the consultation, along with Jack Ruder. The sun was just starting its afternoon descent as they sat on the patio, facing the ocean. After they had traded introductions during the first pot of tea, Father Brown broke the ice.

"So what makes you think I can help you catch this obviously troubled soul?"

"This troubled soul, as you call him, has already killed 16 people." Angela folded her arms and leaned back in her seat.

"Even if he is truly wicked, he is just a man, and, as such, he cannot live forever."

"Just the same, Angela is right. We can't have him out there killing people while we wait for him to die a natural death."

"Of course not, Mr. Marks." Father Brown offered Angela another cup of tea from the steaming pot that the waitress had put on the table. She nodded and he poured. "That brings me back to my original question. I want to help, but you have to tell me how."

"We need a theological consultant. The suspect speaks in Bible verses and he also purports to speak in tongues. I've been consulted as an expert on language, but he's sending messages and, while I feel competent deciphering them, I'm not so comfortable composing responses."

"Messages? As I understand, he's writing them in blood."

"He's also been calling Mr. Marks. It would be good if you could be on hand to tell Mr. Marks how to respond."

Brent related the conversation he had had with Banks after the bus massacre, and played the two taped conversations.

"This conversation you had after the bus murders and the two you recorded seem to be with two different people."

"Or the same person with multiple personality disorder."

"Very possible, Dr. Beverly. Just the same, the first person seemed afraid; the second determined and brave. The first seemed to me to be godly and timid; the second threatening."

"I don't know how godly he could possibly be, but the FBI considers this to be the same suspect."

"Just the same, I may be able to help you communicate with him – get him to reveal more about himself that could help you apprehend him. Do you have a transcript of the conversations?"

"I do." Jack reached into his briefcase. "I made a copy for you and for Dr. Beverly." Jack handed a copy of the report to both of them.

"He says here that he has seen the ancient serpent, the devil. And he calls the devil by some of the names we know him to be called by in different languages, such as 'Azazael' and 'Abaddon'."

"And he told me that Satan had come to him in the form of an angel."

"Yes, that is consistent with scripture. In 2 Corinthians 11:14, Satan disguises himself as an angel of light."

"Then he speaks in tongues."

"Unfortunately, that cannot be verified. He purported to speak in tongues. While there are some Acts of the Apostles that reference speaking in tongues, and also in Corinthians 14:5, it's not a traditional form of prayer in Catholicism."

"Then he says he has been captured by the evil one and brushed with the powers of darkness."

"Yes, and that is where he seems to be showing his fear. He was captured by what he believes to be Satan, who came to him disguised as an angel, and now is asking God to show him the way out."

"Help us catch him, Father, and we'll show him the way out."

"Agent Wollard, I can't assist you in setting a trap to kill this man." Father Brown frowned, and his lips tightened.

"Don't worry, Father. We'll take him alive." She leaned back again. "If we can."

"What about the recorded phone messages, Father?"

"Well, the first is a verse from John 16:13. *'When the Spirit of truth is come, He will guide you into all truth. He will not speak from Himself, but whatever He may hear, He will speak. And He will declare to you the things coming.'*"

"Is he saying to Brent that he's going to tell him what is going to happen next?"

"Yes, Mr. Ruder, that would be my interpretation. In the scripture, of course, we are being told that the Holy Spirit will show us the way. But your suspect is not a prophet. There is only one Christ, and God cannot be speaking through this man. He is using to the scripture to send his own earthly message."

"What about his speaking in tongues after that?"

"I don't recognize that as any language, did you Dr. Beverly?"

"No."

"Well, we know he can't be speaking in tongues, because speaking in tongues is when the Holy Spirit speaks through a human vessel, and there is nothing holy about his acts or deeds."

Angela nodded. "Unholy, if you ask me."

"I think we can all agree on that. Then he says that *an angel hath been revealed to me and will show thee the way*. This doesn't appear to be a quotation of any scripture, per se. The literal meaning of it, I suppose, is that he thinks he is getting some kind of divine instruction and will make some type of revelation to Mr. Marks."

"What about: *It is the glory of God to conceal things and the truth will be revealed in its own time*?"

"Proverbs 25:2: 'It is the glory of God to conceal a thing, but the honor of kings is to search out a matter.' The second verse is not correctly recited, but it sounds like Ecclesiastes 3:1: 'For everything there is a season and a time for every purpose under the heaven.' *It shall be written in blood* has no place in the scriptures, but it could explain his choice of medium for the message."

"Very clinically put, Father. What do you think he's trying to tell us?"

"I suppose, Mr. Marks, that he's trying to tell us that we can expect him to reveal and identify himself when the time has come."

"What time is that?"

"I don't know, Agent Wollard. Only he knows that."

"It seems to me that this man thinks he's doing God's work, in a weird way, and that he wants the message of what he is doing to be spread."

"That's an interesting hypothesis, Dr. Beverly."

"He's trying to cure the world of homosexuality?"

"That's what it would appear, Mr. Marks. And it seems he has chosen you to spread his message."

"Okay, I get that, but what about: *I am outside your dimensions*?"

"This is where I disagree with Dr. Beverly. When we speak of communication with God, since he is outside our dimensions, He cannot speak to us directly. He speaks to us in other ways. This man either thinks he is

108

communicating with God or another spirit who is outside of our dimensions. We know that this is not possible, because the Bible teaches us that the Father, the Son and the Holy Spirit are one."

"What about Satan?"

"Good point, Mr. Ruder. Maybe he believes he is talking to God, or maybe an angel of God, or even Satan. We can't know what's going on in his head. But there's one thing I think we can be sure of."

"What's that?"

"I think he intends to kill again. Where else would he get the blood to write his messages?"

# CHAPTER FIFTEEN

Dr. Beverly convinced Father Brown to go to a
"slumber party" of sorts at Brent's house. In
fact, everyone was invited and, for the first time,
all three of Brent's guest rooms were occupied.
Deputy Salinger was on night duty. He would
monitor the phone and sound the alarm to wake
everyone up if a call was received, so his guest
room was unoccupied for most of the night. Dr.
Beverly and Father Brown took the other two
rooms and, of course, Angela and Brent bunked
together.

"It's kind of weird, don't you think?"

"What?"

"That we're sleeping together in the same room with a priest right downstairs?"

"Angela, you're not Catholic."

"I know, but we're not married."

"And you don't want to sin in the presence of a man of God?"

"Something like that."

"Don't worry, Angie, I don't think sleep is a sin. And we'd better get some of it in case our maniac calls tonight."

When Brent's head hit the pillow, he struggled to find sleep. As he watched the peaceful sleeping face of Angela next to him, he thought that it was the only thing he had seen during the past several weeks that made him feel good.

Just when it seemed that sleep had finally discovered him, he was awakened by Deputy Salinger's alarm. Brent donned his bathrobe and ran to the living room, where he put on his headphone and, on Salinger's cue, answered the phone just as Father Brown appeared at the top of the stairs.

"Hello?"

*"One shall not lie with a male as with a woman. It is an abomination."*

112

Father Brown held his receiver to his ear, and whispered: "Leviticus 18:22."

Angela walked into the room quietly, fastening her gun belt and carrying her flak jacket.

"I do not bear the sword in vain. I am a servant of God who carries out God's wrath on the wrongdoers."

"Ask if he is prepared to perish by the sword."

"Mr. Banks, are you prepared to perish by the sword?"

The sound of laughter echoed eerily throughout the room. "I see there is a holy man with you."

"Ask how he knows."

"How do you know that?"

"We have met before. Remember, Father?"

Father Brown felt a shiver of fear. *Impossible.*

"Ask him to identify himself."

"Who is speaking to me, exactly? Who are you?"

"You have very good counsel. I have many names. And I speak in many tongues. All the tongues of the world. Hen did bady shamu laka ni terra."

"Ask if he is a demon."

"Are you a demon?"

"Nay, I am a spirit."

"What kind of spirit?"

"What kind of spirit?"

"You have the expert counsel. Maybe the good Father can help you decipher my message."

"What…" The phone died again.

"We have a location!" Deputy Salinger radioed the location.

"Give it to me." Angela wrote down the address and headed out the door.

"Angie, where are you going?"

"Don't worry, Brent. I'll have plenty of company. Stay here with Salinger in case he calls again."

\*\*\*

As Angela sped off, she called Tomassi on the special radio frequency that had been established for the task force.

"This is Special Agent Wollard. I am en-route, requesting instructions."

"Detective Tomassi – meet me at 3947 Seafarer Road. We're setting up a command post there with the Ventura County Sheriff's SWAT team."

"Roger that: my ETA is approximately 20 minutes."

\*\*\*

Tomassi was there when Angela arrived, briefing the SWAT Team. Five minutes later, SWAT was breaking down the door to 3920 Seafarer Road. When they got the "all clear" signal, they entered, along with their team of deputies from the Santa Barbara Sheriff's Department. The occupant of the house was home; just not in the same dimension.

Inside, the scene was all too familiar to Angela – but this time there was only one male body, nude and covered in blood, posed on his knees against the wall as if in he were in prayer.

And there was a message on the wall written in blood: *Marks 2013.*

"Again, your boyfriend.   Poor bastard." Tomassi looked down at the lifeless praying statue.

"Maybe Brent holds the key to finding this guy."

"I hate compromising investigations, but I have to agree with you.  Call Salinger and get him on the line."

Brent was on pins and needles, worrying about Angela, until she finally called.

"Brent, we need your help.   There was another murder; this time only one victim, posed like he was praying, and another message left for you: 2013."

"2013?"

"What happened to you in 2013?"

"It couldn't be about me."

"Your name is in the message."

"Still: nothing specific about 2013 comes to mind."

"What about Banks?"

"Nothing that sticks out in my mind about 2013."

Father Brown motioned to Brent. It looked urgent.

"Sorry to interrupt, but I may know something about 2013. How many victims?"

"One."

"And the body was posed, like before?"

"As if in prayer."

Brown looked both worried and excited. "You should be looking for another victim."

Brent regarded Brown with a furrowed brow.

"Father Brown says we should be looking for another victim."

"Father Brown – why? Salinger, could you put us on speakerphone?"

Salinger clicked the speakerphone button for Father Brown's revelation.

"It's Leviticus 20:13: *If a man also lie with mankind, as he lieth with a woman, both of them have committed an abomination: they shall surely be put to death; their blood shall be upon them.*"

Back at the scene, Tomassi turned to the deputies from the Ventura County Sheriff's Department.

"I need a full sweep of the neighborhood. If the perp is still here somewhere, let's get him. Stop and detain anyone you see who looks suspicious and call me."

Four of the deputies turned at Tomassi's command.

"Wait: we also need to see if the victim registered for a same-sex marriage."

"You'll have to wait until the clerk opens at 8 a.m."

"Whoever the next victim is, he doesn't have until 8 a.m."

# CHAPTER SIXTEEN

Angela answered her cell phone on speaker amid the chaos at the latest crime scene. She was standing right next to Tomassi.

"Angie, have you got an identity on the victim?"

Tomassi butted in: "We can't divulge that information, Marks."

"Then you'd better bring more mops and buckets, because you'll be cleaning up another bloody murder scene. I can have Jack Ruder on this in two seconds."

"Sorry, Marks. You'll have to wait until it's released to the public, like everyone else. We've got it."

"Angie? You good with that?"

"Detective Tomassi is the lead detective on this case. I can't go against his directive."

"Suit yourselves."

\*\*\*

Brent waited for Deputy Salinger to take a bathroom break, then surreptitiously glanced at his notebook while holding up his finger to his lips, giving Father Brown the "shh" sign.

"Got it." Brent noted the address in his notebook, whipped out his cell phone, and called Jack as he walked back into the bedroom to change.

"Jack, I've got an emergency."

"You sure as hell better have one at five in the morning."

Brent cradled the cell phone with his cheek, pressing against it with his shoulder as he slipped on his pants.

"There's been another murder; this time only one victim, but the killer left a bible verse indicating he was after his partner."

"I'm not sure if they were engaged or what, but they're not together anymore. This guy's in real danger. We have to find him."

Brent gave Jack the address. "Do a full background check on the victim. Find out any significant relationships. We have to track them all down. And meet me at the office as soon as you've got a lead. I'm on my way now."

Brent quickly finished dressing and headed out the door.

"Where are you going?"

"To work, Salinger."

"Detective Tomassi said he needs you here in case the guy calls back."

"Father Brown can handle it." Father Brown smiled and nodded.

"Wait! You can't leave!"

"It's my house, Salinger. So, unless you've got a warrant for my arrest or something, I'm outta here. The donuts are in the kitchen."

Salinger stood up, fidgeted, then sat back down, frowning as he watched Brent leave through the front door.

***

The task force's forensics team was called to the scene, but the Ventura County Medical Examiner had jurisdiction over the body. Tomassi called Dr. Perez in to consult. He was on his way and would be there in about half an hour.

The Ventura Medical Examiner reported preliminary results of multiple stab wounds as the cause of death, which had occurred approximately one hour before. He walked the crime scene with Tomassi and agreed to have his team delay removal of the body until Perez could examine it.

***

In less than an hour, Jack met Brent at the office. He was proudly shaking a paper in his hand. "I've got a list."

"A list?"

"Brent, this guy was busy."

"He ever married?"

"Nope."

"He ever engaged?"

"No. But he had a lot of relationships."

"Define *a lot*."

"Nine. And all in the past two years."

"Nine?"

Jack nodded.

"Let's get to work, then. You got phone numbers?"

"Of course."

"Good. Let's split 'em up. I'll call half and you call half."

"Good morning, Mr. Smith, there's a serial killer outside your door waiting to stab you 21 times?"

"Yeah, something like that. Got to get the information to them if we're going to help."

"And the cops?"

"Do you have the list in electronic format?"

"Yes."

"Good. Send it to Angela right away so she'll have it on her phone."

"I wouldn't want to be you when she finds out we've been calling these guys."

"I know, right? I'll put on another pot of coffee."

\*\*\*

After about half an hour of terrifying the men on the list, Brent reached the last name on his – Gerald Portren.

"Mr. Portren?"

There was silence on the line, then: "Mr. Marks? I see the good Father has interpreted my message."

Brent motioned to Jack, who picked up the extra line. Brent pointed to the name, and made the telephone sign with his hand.

"Is Portren still alive?"

"No, Mr. Marks. He's been made to pay for his abomination."

Jack got on his cell phone and placed two calls; one to 9-1-1 emergency and the other to Angela.

"Everyone else has been warned. They're out of your reach."

"Mr. Marks, what do you think? If a man has a hundred sheep, and one of them has gone astray, does he not leave the ninety-nine in the mountains and go in search of the one that went astray?"

A pause, then: "Why have you not shared my lessons with the world?"

"What do you mean?"

"I see nothing in the newspapers or on TV about the punishments; nothing about my messages. The wind blows where it wishes, and you shall hear its sound, but you will not know where it comes from or where it goes."

The line went dead – as dead as Gerald Portren surely was.

# CHAPTER SEVENTEEN

The new murder site was in Oxnard, about ten minutes from the Ventura location. Brent dreaded telling Angela that he had discovered the next victim – now that it was too late to save him – so he had Jack do it. Tomassi called the Oxnard PD to let them know he was on his way, but this time he didn't intend to wait for their SWAT team.

Tomassi took three SBSD patrol cars, which rolled to the scene with him with lights and no siren. He left Angela and Salas in charge of the Ventura scene. After a quick observation and assessment of the entire surrounding area, the deputies formed a perimeter at Tomassi's command, and he approached the front door with two of them. It was ajar. Tomassi's nerves were on the edge, supercharged with adrenalin.

Tomassi motioned to the two deputies for light, and one of them blasted the entry with light while the second raised his shotgun as backup. Tomassi breeched the front door, shotgun ready, looking first to the left, then to the right. He signaled with his head for the deputy to enter after him. He flipped on the lights, making as little surface contact as possible with the switch, so as not to destroy any latent prints. He found himself standing in the living room. A body lay in a pool of blood before him. On the wall, written in blood, were the numbers *12627.*

Tomassi knelt down by the dead man and felt his skin. It was warm. He checked his carotid artery for a pulse, even though he knew he wouldn't find one.

Still silent, and followed by the deputy, Tomassi performed a thorough cursory search of the house. He traversed the blood trail in the corridor, being careful not to disturb any evidence as he examined each room.

As in the first case, the blood trail led to a master bedroom with a blood-soaked mattress, blankets and sheets. There did not appear to have been a struggle, and he was yet to find any evidence of forced entry.

Once Tomassi determined it was safe, he gave the deputies the order to tape off the scene and he put his rubber gloves on. He divided the room into grids and worked outward from the body. The forensics team was still busy at the Ventura location. It was going to be a long day.

As much as he dreaded it, he determined that he would have to call Brent Marks (or at least Father Brown) to get a read on the numbers written on the wall. He figured they were probably more Bible verses. He radioed Deputy Salinger.

"Salinger, is Father Brown still there?"

"Yes, sir. He's here."

"Put him on."

Salinger handed his radio to Father Brown and showed him where to push to talk.

"This is Father Brown. How can I help you, Detective?"

"We have another victim."

"Oh, my!" Father Brown hung his head dolefully, his eyebrows drawn together as he crossed himself.

"He left another message on the wall, in blood."

"What does it say?"

"All numbers – 12627."

"12627? No spaces, colons?"

"No, just 12627."

Father Brown put his hand on his chin. *12627, 126, 12, 62, 7.*

"I'm sorry, Detective Tomassi, but I'm going to need some more time on this one."

"Take your time, Father. I'm going to be at this for a while."

He would start with the Old Testament, as that was where the other verses had come from. Father Brown reached into his satchel for his favorite Bible. Given to him by Father Ignatius (a senior Franciscan monk, when Brown was a young man studying in the seminary), it had been a useful guide all his life. But he never thought he would be using it to help solve a crime.

Father Brown carefully flipped through the delicate pages, starting with the first book of the Old Testament – Genesis 1:26-27.

*That seems to apply. Let us make mankind in our image – male and female. No, that can't be it.*

*It's not in Leviticus. Maybe the New Testament. What does the New Testament say about homosexuality?*

"Romans 1:26-27!" Father Brown beamed, then realized that his sudden burst of pride was a sin, and crossed himself.

"What?" Salinger looked confused.

"Romans 1:26-27! Right here in the New Testament! Deputy, please get Detective Tomassi on the line."

Brown took the bible from his sack and out of its cloth pouch. He ran his fingers over the gold leaf titles, thought of Ignatius briefly, and turned to the book of Romans.

"Here it is: *For this reason God gave them up to dishonorable passions. For their women exchanged natural relations for those that are contrary to nature. And the men likewise gave up natural relations with women and were consumed with passion for one another, men committing shameless acts with men and receiving in themselves due penalty for their error.*"

Deputy Salinger radioed for Tomassi.

"Father Brown for you, sir."

He handed his radio to Brown, who could not mask his excitement. It was the predominant feeling in the emotional cocktail along with grief, disbelief and sadness.

"Detective Tomassi? I believe the killer's next victim will be a woman."

# CHAPTER EIGHTEEN

Angela and Rhonda Salas played their investigation by the book as the forensics team completed their tasks at the Ventura scene. There were no signs of a struggle and the victim, as in the other case, appeared to have been killed in bed, then dragged to the living room and posed. On the floor in the living room, they found a wad of paper with torn edges that was covered in blood, and left it there to be photographed, cataloged and secured.

They logged in personal possessions that she had found in the bedroom – a man's gold watch, a wallet filled with credit cards, and $225.00 in cash, bracelets, camera equipment, and a coin collection. Robbery was not a motive in this case, as in the others. A profile was emerging; unfortunately, at the expense of more lives.

Dr. Perez was just finishing his secondary examination of the body when Tomassi called. Two Sergeants - Dean Johnson and Harold

Jenner, who had been assigned to the task force from the Santa Barbara County Sheriff's Department - lifted 45 latent fingerprints. The Medical Examiner would take foot and finger prints of the victim. The prints were sent off to be matched against the FBI's database.

"Wollard, can you leave Salas in charge and get over here right away? I need you over here."

"I'll be there right away. And I'll bring Dr. Perez with me."

"Yeah, I need him too."

Tomassi escaped the smell of copper and blood at the death scene into the fresh air outside. He opened the door of his car, sat on the seat with his legs dangling out, and rested his elbows on his knees and his forehead in his hands. He made a sound that was somewhere between a groan and a sigh as the frustration and fatigue overcame him.

A Sherriff's Deputy who was walking by stopped in front of him. "Detective, are you all right?"

He waved him off. "Yes, Deputy, I'm fine."

When Angela arrived, Detective Tomassi toured the crime scene with her and then briefed her on Father Brown's theory of who would be the next victim of the Honeymoon Stalker.

"We can't assume anymore that his intended victims are participants in same-sex marriages. This victim, Gerald Portren, was an ex-boyfriend of the last victim."

"And now Father Brown thinks the next victim will be a woman."

"Yes. What are we supposed to do now? Look up every gay woman in Santa Barbara and Ventura Counties?"

"Obviously, we don't have the data or the manpower for that." Angela sighed. "But we can't give up. There must be a clue to follow here somewhere. We just have to find it."

The Ventura Medical Examiner as well as Dr. Perez had finished their examination of the body.

"I don't have to tell you, Rolly, that the cause of death was multiple stab wounds: approximately a six- to seven-inch blade. Looks like the work of the same killer."

"And the time of death?"

"Within the last two hours."

By this time, a considerable amount of spectators had arrived. Tomassi pulled aside one of the photographers. "Make sure you get detailed pictures of the crowd."

***

Brent and Jack had hit a dead end. They decided to go back to Brent's place and take Father Brown out to breakfast to pick his brain. They stopped by Spudnuts on the way home to pick up some fresh donuts and coffee for Salinger.

When they entered the house, Brent put the box of donuts and steaming coffee in front of the deputy.

"Thanks, guys." Salinger opened the donut box and looked at the sticky, spongy selection of sugar-glazed American pastries. "Uh, this isn't all for me, is it?"

"Bon appétit!" Brent waved to Salinger and he, Jack, and Father Brown left.

"Hey, where are you guys going?"

"Let's just say some of us don't do donuts."

***

He stepped into the shower, turned on the water, and let the hot jets pummel his blood-soaked body. Red water cascaded from his hair, down his chest and legs, and swirled in a whirlpool at the drain. He opened his mouth and tasted the blood as it poured from his head. He spit and looked down. He was hard again, and he began to masturbate.

He felt overwhelmed with shame and guilt. *I am a servant of the Lord. This is His work. Why should I be so excited? It is a sin. I must cleanse myself.*

He lathered the washrag and scrubbed his skin until it was as red as the water. "I believe in God, the Father Almighty, creator of heaven and earth!

"And in Jesus Christ, His only Son, our Lord; who was conceived by the Holy Spirit, born of the Virgin Mary!"

He prayed until his swelling subsided, then emerged from the shower, invigorated and angry. *The unholy woman is next. She who uses her body in an unnatural manner.*

\*\*\*

Andersen's on State Street was a quaint bakery and café with the quaint feel of the California/Danish village of Solvang about it. They settled at a table inside, near the window, and ordered breakfast.

"Father, this lunatic is killing people and using the word of God not only as his excuse, but as his mandate. Something's wrong here."

"It's true that the Old Testament said that if a man shall lie with another man, both shall be put to death; but you have to remember the context in which that passage was written. Life was very harsh in Old Testament times for the Israelites. They did not have prisons, and stoning to death was the penalty for many crimes."

Father Brown explained to them why he thought the next victim would be a woman.

"The Old Testament mainly spoke about homosexual relations between men being a sin. There was nothing mentioned about female homosexuality. But the New Testament has some verses in Romans that have been interpreted that way by some biblical scholars."

"Well, how can you interpret it one way or the other? I mean, doesn't it say what it says?"

"You have to remember that the Bible was written many years ago, in Greek, at different times, and by different authors."

"I'm Jewish, so it's all Greek to me."

"Very funny, Jack. Go on, Father."

"Saint Paul most likely wrote the book of Romans, and in it, Romans 1:26-27 discusses the subject of sexuality. Those were the verses referred to on the wall of the last victim.

"It talks about women giving up natural relations for those that are unnatural, and men giving up relations with women in favor of those with one another."

"So, he's after a gay woman now?"

"I think so."

"The question is *who*?"

# CHAPTER NINETEEN

There were four crime scenes, now, to analyze. Latent prints lifted from the bus murder matched only the prisoners who were still in custody and the three SBSD deputies and, of course, Joshua Banks, who was still the primary suspect. The attacking truck had been reported stolen and was found, but there were no latents at all found inside – not even smudges – which indicated that the driver was either wearing gloves, wiped it clean, or both. Blood types from the bus were matched to the victims. No blood identified as Banks' was found on the scene.

Since the bus murder was a different case under different circumstances and didn't fit the pattern, the task force decided to concentrate on the murders that had occurred at the homes in Santa Barbara, Ventura and Oxnard. They had the full resources of the FBI's data bases and laboratory services to assist them in their investigation, and gained more manpower from the Santa Barbara and Ventura County Sheriff's Departments. They had compiled a full psychological profile on the killer, whom they assumed to be Banks.

Detective Tomassi left Salas in charge of the Ventura case while he and Angela worked the Oxnard case for clues. A total of 36 latent prints were taken from the scene and samples from the blood in the bedroom and living room, as well as the carpet in the corridor, were obtained for typing and DNA analysis.

"We'll have to wait for the data matching reports on the blood and the prints. I made a full sweep here and didn't find anything. No sign of forced entry, no sign of a struggle, no weapon. It's like he sneaks in with a key or something and attacks them in their sleep."

"He must have disarmed the alarms. The other two houses had them."

"Maybe one of your electronic experts can take a look at them."

"I'll get them on it. I'll work the scene after they remove the body. Can I have your log?"

Tomassi handed her his log book. "Great. I'll go back over to Ventura and help Salas wrap up things there. We can meet after and compare notes."

"We should put the whole team on alert to keep their radios on them at all times. We have to be prepared to roll on a moment's notice."

"Good idea, Wollard."

After Tomassi left, Angela went over his notes and discussed the case with the officers on duty and the forensics team. She walked through the scene carefully. *You must have left something behind.*

After the body was removed and the photographers and print experts had finished their jobs, she walked the entire house, checking everything. She double checked the front door, which had been left ajar - probably by the killer. It didn't appear to have been locked and there were no latent prints that had been found on it. Portren did not have an alarm system. She checked the sliding glass doors and back door for evidence of forced entry. Like Tomassi, she found none; but the back door had no deadbolt, and although it was locked, it could have easily been opened with a credit card.

She inspected all the windows and took note of the type of curtains and drapes. She examined the kitchen. All in all, the kitchen was in pretty good shape. Portren had been a good housekeeper. *No visible blood.* She shone her bright UV light on the sink and could see that it had already been treated with fluorescein. There were traces of blood, which meant that the killer had probably cleaned at least his hands here. There was no visible sign of blood at the front door area, which they presumed was the point of exit.

No cigarettes, butts, or ashtrays. Portren must have not been a smoker. She examined the blood spatters in the master bedroom, sketched them, and took her own photographs to scale. She looked under the bed and mattress to ascertain if anything had been hidden there.

After Angela had examined the entire house thoroughly, she looked at the property outside. In the backyard, she carefully searched for any signs that the killer may have used the back or sliding glass doors to enter or exit. In the front, which she and Tomassi concluded was the exit path, she found what appeared to be a few drops of blood, photographed them, and made sure the forensic team got samples for testing.

The Seafarer Road location was still buzzing with activity, even though most of the forensics team was already in Oxnard. Salas had done the same thorough examination of the interior and exterior of the house.

\*\*\*

"Jack, you should go over all the databases you can to see if Banks ever threatened any gay woman."

"I thought you didn't think Banks was our guy."

"Well, he hasn't surfaced since the bus killings, has he?"

"No."

"Then, if he's not our guy, in order to help him, we have to try to catch him. And if he's the killer, that'll help Angela and her team as well."

"And if he's not?"

"Then he has a lot of explaining to do."

# CHAPTER TWENTY

When Rhonda Salas finally got back home that night, she was exhausted. She hung up her jacket and secured her gun in the gun safe in the bedroom closet, then went into the kitchen to see what there was to eat. She opened the refrigerator and looked inside. *Great. Last week's leftovers.* She couldn't remember when she had last enjoyed a home-cooked meal, but certainly didn't have the energy to cook one tonight. She found some tomatoes and cucumbers that didn't look too old, and took them out to make a salad. There were some chicken legs in one of the leftover containers, so she threw them into the microwave.

After dinner, Rhonda decided to treat herself to a luxurious hot bath. First she straightened up a bit, chucking some dirty clothes from the hamper into the washing machine and starting a load of wash. Then she ran the bath with a generous amount of salts, pushing the water with her hand and adjusting the temperature until it was perfect. She shed her bra and panties and immersed herself into the comforting swirl of bubbles and hot water, sighing in relief. *Just what I need. It feels so good.*

Even though she was off work, she couldn't help but think about the case. Hopefully something would come back from the lab with a DNA analysis or a print match that they could use for a lead.

Even though Tomassi was convinced it was Joshua Banks, she wasn't so sure. How could a blowhard like him turn into a calculated killing machine that seemed to leave no identifiable clues behind? *It's like we're chasing a ghost.* And there was the religious angle which, when mixed with homophobia, gave the case another dimension of terror. She herself was a recovering Catholic and could never escape the memory of her father pointing his finger at her and calling her a sinner when she finally confessed to her parents that she had come out.

\*\*\*

When Brent finally gave in and called Angela, he received a cold reception at the end of the line.

"How many times have we discussed not interfering with active investigations?"

"I'm sorry, Angie, but I still have a client with a chunk of retainer money sitting in my trust account. Technically, I not only have the right, but also the obligation to pursue my own investigation."

"You should have at least informed me so I could have set up a proper sting."

"Why don't you come over and we can discuss it?"

A pause on the phone, then: "Why don't *you* come over and we don't discuss it?"

"Let's not and say we did?"

"Something like that."

"Sounds like a good invitation. I'll be right over."

\*\*\*

Rhonda finally sank between the sheets for a well-deserved night's rest, but she still couldn't sleep. Visions of the bloody crime scenes flashed through her head all night, and it seemed like she slept with one eye open.

In the middle of the night, that eye did open just in time to see a shadow moving in the corridor, illuminated by the moonlight. *Am I dreaming? No! Somebody's in the house! No time to get my gun. Think! Think!* She hit the panic button on her radio extension, which was clipped to the extra pillow on her bed just as the figure appeared at her door.

He came at her fast, and she kicked him in the groin, which caused the knife to land off-target, cutting into her left shoulder. Crying out in pain, she rolled out of the way, grabbed the pillow and deflected his next stab, which exploded feathers all over the room.

"The cops are coming, motherfucker!"

He hesitated, which allowed her to get a good look at him. He was wearing a black sweater and had on a mask. There was no way to identify him. *He's going to cut me again! But I have to keep moving!* Then he lunged at her again. She hunched her back, moving out of harm's way as he swiped the knife in front of her midsection, then grabbed his wrist with her right hand and hit the back of his hand as hard as she could with her left, and heard the knife fall to the floor. Then Rhonda ran for her life. She ran out into the corridor and headed for the front door. She felt the warmth of the blood dripping from her shoulder wound but couldn't think about doing anything about it. She had to get out of there.

***

Tomassi had fallen asleep, fully clothed, on his couch, and responded to the panic call right away. He lived about five minutes away from Rhonda's by car. He was first at the scene, where he found her running down her street in what used to be a white nightgown, now in a bloody shade of pink. He quickly opened the door, and she got in.

"Rhonda, I…"

"Go get him! He could still be in the house!"

Tomassi handed his handgun to Rhonda, took the shotgun from the gun rack and ran to the house, just as two VCSD cars and two Santa Barbara PD black and whites pulled up.

Tomassi quickly gave them instructions. Four officers went into the backyard and the entire front was illuminated with blasts of light from the patrol cars.

He burst into the house, with two deputies in tow, blasting his path with light. As the other deputies watched the perimeter, Tomassi ran through each room, looking for the attacker. He found a back door to the house was open, and called for the deputies.

Three more SBPD cars and two sheriff's vehicles came screeching up to join the manhunt. They formed a grid, working out from the house with two SBPD units covering the streets and the rest of the officers canvassing the neighborhood on Tomassi's instructions as his team searched through the back yards for the killer's escape route.

Angela pulled up to Detective Tomassi's car and found Rhonda lying down in it, holding Tomassi's weapon. She had lost a lot of blood. Angela called the Fire Department, put pressure on the wound to stop the bleeding, and tied it with her shirt. She covered Rhonda with her jacket like a blanket.

"Hang in there, Rhonda: help is on the way."

Rhonda blinked and moaned.

"Don't try to talk, just relax. The paramedics are coming."

And Angela waited with Rhonda for help to arrive. Waited and prayed that Rhonda wouldn't be the next victim of the Honeymoon Stalker.

# CHAPTER TWENTY ONE

Tomassi took off on a hunch and decided to follow the distant sounds of the barking dogs, which seemed to set a pattern. *He must be going through back yards. Toward the park!*

Tomassi punched the button on his radio as he ran. "Davis, I think he's headed for the park. Get units on Arrelaga, Santa Barbara, Garden, Sola and Anacapa. Surround the park."

"Copy."

\*\*\*

He heard them in the distance as he emerged from the bushes.

*They think I'm in the park.*

He opened the door to the old car and climbed in. His pride ached more than his groin, which was uncomfortable. He had underestimated the woman. Still, she had been chosen.

*It must be God's will that she lived.*

He had to put the second plan into action. This part of the job had been finished; just not the way he thought it would be. He pulled out on Victoria and headed toward State Street. That would be the best place to blend in.

A couple of police cars rushed by him, headed the other way, their lights blazing. *Probably on their way to surround the park.* God had given him the gift of super intelligence to accomplish these tasks, but he didn't understand why He had decided to let her live. *His word is not to question.*

As he turned left on State Street, he blended in with the early morning traffic. State Street was Santa Barbara's main street. They wouldn't be looking for him there. He would hide from them in plain sight.

Suddenly, as he passed Anapamu, the inside of his car was illuminated from the reflection of the red light in his rear view mirror. He reached for the gun in his glove box and tucked it under his butt, just in case.

The officer approached, and tipped his hat.

"Good morning, sir."

"Good morning."

"May I see your license and registration, please?"

He presented his license and the papers from the old car. The officer shone his light on them and then looked at him. He kept his hand ready to go for the gun.

"Do you know why I stopped you, sir?"

"No, officer, but I'm running late for work. Is it something serious?"

"Well it could be. Your right brake light is out. I'm going to write you a fix-it ticket. You won't have to pay anything if you just replace the light and show us proof at the station."

"Is it going to take a long time?"

The officer smiled. "Not long at all. I'll be right back."

He watched in the rear-view as the officer walked back to his motorcycle.

*Why isn't he joining the chase?*

Two more police cars with lights blaring whipped past him in the opposite direction. Then the officer came running back to the car. He gripped the gun with his right hand as he watched in the mirror.

"You're lucky, sir. I've been called to an emergency. Get that light fixed, now." He handed his papers back and ran back to his motorcycle.

***

Joshua Banks woke up. It was dark. He was sweating profusely. He was on a couch in a room he didn't recognize. He tried to get up, but his head was spinning and he fell back onto the couch. *What's happening to me? What is God trying to tell me?* For so long, he had been in the possession of the evil thing, the agent of Satan, Azazel himself. Now he looked around the room, but the evil spirit was nowhere to be found. But the room was spinning just as surely as if he were in the center of a carousel. He crawled to the edge of the whirling room to get off, and when he saw the opportunity, he jumped.

Joshua was naked. He looked around the place and saw a pile of clothes. He rifled through them for pants and a shirt. There was only one shirt and one pair of pants, right on top of the pile. The dizziness brought on a bout of nausea, but he couldn't throw up. He sat on the floor until the spinning in his head stopped. Then, he put on the pants and shirt. He was between dimensions, and couldn't tell where the physical world ended and the spiritual world began. *Help me Lord! Help your child find his way home!* He dropped to his knees and prayed, and the Lord provided him with shoes, which he found near the pile of clothes. He put them on and looked for a way out.

He whispered, so the evil spirit would not hear him, "God, show me, your poor pilgrim, the way home!"

And God showed him the door. He opened it, and he was finally free. And Joshua Banks ran. He didn't know where he was, or where he was going, but he knew he had to get as far as he could away from that evil place.

He looked up at the sky. The stars were whirling around – as if God had created a tornado in space. Then he drove away. He wasn't sure if he was in his car or not. Maybe he was. Maybe he wasn't. Anyway: car or not, he drove toward home.

After a while, he was tired. He couldn't be in his car. He was confused. He didn't know where he was or how to get home. He found a public phone booth, and dialed 0 for the Operator.

"Operator, how can I help you?"

Banks couldn't think of what to say.

"This is the Operator."

"I'm in trouble. I need to get home."

"Do you want to call somebody?"

"Yes, yes. I want to call somebody."

"Who do you want to call?"

He thought for a moment. "I don't know!"

"Sir, you must know who you want to call."

"Yes! Yes! My counselor at law: Marks, Brent. Brent Marks. I want to call him!"

"What is his number?"

"I don't know." He began to cry.

"Is he a local attorney? In Santa Barbara?"

"Yes! Yes!" Banks sobbed.

"Brent Marks, on State Street?"

"Yes! That's him! Thank God you found him!"

"How do you want to pay for the call?"

"What call?"

"Is this a collect call or can you pay with coins or a credit card?"

"It's an emergency! I need to speak with Counselor Marks."

"Collect, then?"

"Yes, yes!"

"Whom shall I say is calling?"

"Whom is calling? I am calling. It's me."

"What is your name?"

"Joshua Banks."

The Operator called through to Brent, and he accepted the charges.

"You are connected."

"Mr. Banks?"

"Yes, it is I. I have escaped from the demon."

"Where are you?"

"I don't know!" He sobbed and sniffed.

"Mr. Banks. Look outside. Do you see a street sign?"

"Yes, yes there is a sign. Thank God!"

"What does it say?"

"It says State Street."

"That's good. Is there a number on it?"

"Yes."

"What number?"

"I can't see it."

"Look closer, then."

"2520."

"Stay there, I'll come and get you. But you have to turn yourself in, do you understand?"

Banks pondered the question. "Turn myself into what?"

"Mr. Banks, every cop in town is looking for you now. If you don't turn yourself in to the police, they will kill you for sure."

"Whatever you say. I am waiting for you, counselor. I don't know where I am, but I am waiting."

Joshua Banks slid down against the back of the phone booth and hit the ground, his head still spinning furiously.

"Dear God, make it stop! Make it stop!"

# CHAPTER TWENTY TWO

Brent called Jack to help him recover Joshua Banks.  He would call Angela when they had secured him.  No need for a manhunt to end with police shooting up a phone booth like Bonnie and Clyde.  Banks was obviously deranged, on drugs, or both.  *I didn't even know they had phone booths anymore.*

"Meet me at State and Constance.  Don't approach him until I'm there.  He could be very dangerous."

"Okay."

"And, Brent…"

"Yes?"

"Take your gun."

When Brent arrived at State and Constance, he saw Jack's car at the corner. It looked a lot like an unmarked police car. *What a surprise.* Brent pulled up alongside him and rolled down the window.

"I'll take the left side and you take the right side. When you see him, call me."

"Jack, this isn't a sting operation."

"Brent…"

"Okay, okay. I'll call you."

"And if you see him, wait for me."

"Yes, mother."

Brent slowly went down State Street, looking at the right side. He reached the phone booth, but there was no sign of Banks. He called Jack.

"Jack, I found the phone booth, but nobody's there."

"Did you cover your side on the whole block?"

"Yes. Nothing."

"I'll be right there. Stay in your car."

Jack pulled up behind Brent, got out of his car, gun drawn, and approached the phone booth cautiously. He kicked the accordion door to the phone booth open, then called Brent.

"All clear. Let's cover the next block, the same way."'

Brent carefully trolled the following block. They were assuming that Banks would walk toward downtown, where he lived, but there could be no guarantee of that, because he seemed to be so out of it.

Brent saw a drunk street bum staggering down the sidewalk on the right hand side. He slowed down to get a good look at him. *It's Banks!*

"Jack, I've found him! Do you see me?"

"Yes, I'm coming. Don't approach him without me!"

Brent hung back and waited for Jack as Banks staggered down the street. Jack swung a U-turn and pulled up behind Brent. He ran to Brent's car and leaned up against the door.

"Okay, this is how we're going to play it. He doesn't know me, so you'll have to approach him first. I'll hang back and cover you, but if he makes an aggressive move, drop to the ground and I'll take him out."

"Jack!"

"I'm serious Brent. This could be the most infamous serial killer in Santa Barbara history and your life isn't worth giving up for one of your hunches."

"Okay, okay."

"And don't get within striking range of him. Plus, he may have a gun. If he makes one aggressive move, I have to put him down."

Brent agreed and approached Banks, going a bit faster than his pace so he could catch up to him, but not too fast so as to freak him out. When he got close enough for Banks to hear him, he called to him.

"Mr. Banks, it's Brent Marks. I came, just like you said."

Banks turned his head to look at Brent, then began to run. Brent turned to yell at Jack.

"Jack, don't shoot!" He turned back and pursued Banks. "Mr. Banks, it's Counselor Marks. God sent me!"

Banks stopped suddenly, and turned around.

"God sent you?"

"Yes. This is Counselor Marks. I've been sent by God to bring you to safety."

"Oh, Saints be praised!" Banks cried and dropped to the concrete on his knees, folding his hands in prayer and looking toward the heavens.

"Thank you, Lord, thank you!"

As Brent approached Banks, Jack moved behind him. Brent felt hit by a wall of noxious and repulsive smells. Banks was emaciated and, except for the full gray beard, his face looked like a skull with caved-in cheeks, like Edward Munch's "The Scream." He smelled of the pungent stench of body odor with a touch of shit, urine, and vomit thrown on top. Brent resisted his gag reflex.

"Mr. Banks, this is my friend, Jack Ruder. God sent him to help us."

"I am thankful, Lord for everything! You have truly set me free and given me joy unspeakable!"

Jack helped Banks up, frisking him.

"He's clean."

"Counselor, I have been the prisoner of a most foul demon."

Banks was wearing black pants and a black sweatshirt that matched the description that Salas had given of her attacker's clothes, but they seemed baggy and oversized on Banks. They were smelly, stiff and had dried dark splotches of something on them.

"An unclean spirit who speaks in strange tongues and who slays people in the name of God!"

"That's blood on his clothes, Brent. And you don't have to guess that it's not his."

Brent looked back at Jack and nodded. "Sit with him in the back, Brent. I'll drive."

Brent helped Banks into Jack's car.

"Come on, Mr. Banks. Remember, I told you that you have to turn yourself in to the police?"

"The police?"

"Yes, they're trying to stop the demon. You'll be safe there, and then I can help you. I can't help you unless we go to the police."

"Counselor, if God hath sent you, pray lead the way." Banks staggered on his feet and Brent caught him from falling.

"First, I want the doctor to check you out."

"Yes, Counselor. I'm dizzy." Banks began babbling to himself again.

"What doctor?"

"I'm going to call Orozco to do a blood test."

"What for?"

"I think he's on some kind of drugs or something."

"I think he belongs in the looney bin."

"That, too." Brent pulled out his iPhone and made the call.

"Doc? It's Brent Marks."

"Brent? What time is it?"

"It's early, Doc. Sorry, but I've got an urgent matter. I need you."

"What is it?"

"A blood test."

"Brent, anyone can draw blood. Go to emergency hospital."

"This one's different."

"How so?"

"It's Joshua Banks."

"Bring him right over. I'll meet you at the office."

When Jack and Brent presented Banks to Orozco, he almost didn't take the blood sample.

"This man needs medical attention. He's dehydrated. I'll put him on an IV immediately."

"Doc, we really can't alter his condition in any way. Just take his blood. We can give him some water to drink."

***

After the short stop at Orozco's office, Jack drove to the Sheriff's headquarters on Calle Real as Brent called Angela.

"Angie, it's me."

"Brent, why are you calling so early?"

"Joshua Banks just turned himself in to me, and Jack and I are taking him to the Sheriff's station."

"Oh my God!"

"Can you call Tomassi?"

"Yes, yes, of course, Brent. And I'll be right down there as soon as I can get dressed."

"Great. Tell Tomassi to handle him gently. He's out of it, on some kind of drugs."

"I will."

They pulled up to the station, exited the car, and walked in with Joshua Banks. Jack looked so much like a cop and was holding Banks by the arm, so it appeared to be normal. The Desk Deputy looked up, disinterested.

"What can I help you with, sir?"

"I'm Jack Ruder, private investigator, and this is attorney Brent Marks. We've brought in Joshua Banks to surrender to Detective Tomassi."

The Deputy's eyes opened up like two full moons. "That's Banks?"

"My client is turning himself in. He's unarmed and will cooperate."

The Deputy hit the intercom. "Call Tomassi and get the Lieutenant out here right away! We've got Joshua Banks!"

Banks looked around, confused. "Is this the house of God?"

*More like the house of pain.*

# CHAPTER TWENTY THREE

Sheriff Clayton Thomas proudly stood in front of the podium in the room crowded with reporters who were holding microphones with the logos of their media outlets, among dozens of cameras and video cameras.

Sheriff Thomas ran his fingers through his handlebar moustache and cleared his throat. "Good morning, ladies and gentlemen. I'm pleased to announce to you that we've recaptured Joshua Banks."

A female reporter in the front line thrust her microphone forward. "Is Joshua Banks your primary suspect in the Honeymoon Stalker case?"

"The investigation in that case is ongoing, so I can't disclose any details. I want to give my sincere thanks to the task force team of local and federal law enforcement who made this moment possible. That is all for now. We will be providing updates."

The reporters all perked up with questions like a nest of baby birds peeping for worms.

"But wasn't the focus of the investigation on Banks?"

"He's a suspect in the case. But his arrest is for the murder of Ronald and James Bennett. That's all for now." Thomas stepped down from the podium.

A male reporter from the News Press raised his voice louder than the others.

"Sheriff Thomas, now that you have Banks, will the Honeymoon Stalker case be focusing on him as the primary suspect?"

Thomas was already out the door.

\*\*\*

The following day, Brent met with Banks at the attorney's visiting room at the jail. He appeared to be in better health (at least he was hydrated), and wasn't speaking in tongues. The trouble was that Joshua Banks' regular speech was almost as confusing.

"Counselor, I have met the demon and he is a most evil spirit, I can assure you."

Brent leaned in to Banks, who, thankfully, didn't stink anymore.

"Can you describe this demon?"

"At first I thought he was an angel, come to save me. He looked at me from the heavens. Then he unleashed an evil violence and killed everyone on the bus."

Banks started to cry. "One by one, he slew each of the earthbound sufferers. Then he came to me, and I thought he would kill me too. I said a final prayer and prepared to meet my maker."

"What did he look like?"

"He appeared then in his human form, but after time, he revealed his true appearance. He stood over me, at least 18 feet tall and covered with eyes. He lifted me out with his hands with incredible power."

"Okay, so he's 18 feet tall."

"Yes!"

"What else?"

"He is part animal, part man. He has horns protruding from the sides of his head. He kept me as his prisoner. But then, one day, he vanished and I was saved."

"I'm going to send a friend of mine to talk to you, Mr. Banks. His name is Father Brown."

"Why?"

"Let's just say I think he may be able to help you with your demons."

Banks stared back with a blank look. If Brent wasn't sure before he interviewed Banks whether he would put him on the witness stand to tell his story, he was positive now. He could not testify.

\*\*\*

At the re-arraignment of Joshua Banks on the murder charges of James and Ronald Bennett, Brent had to swim though an ocean of press to get to the courthouse. When he opened the door to the crowded courtroom, he was met right away by the accusing eyes of Susan Fredericks. Her look left no need to say anything verbally. *I know, I'm a scumbag.*

Joshua Banks sat in the jury box alone, under heavy security. His case would be called before any of the other defendants in custody, who were all still in the holding cells. He looked like a lost dog, peering around the courtroom as if it were the first time he had ever seen it. Even Judge Hendron ("Uncle Burt") tried to turn his emoticon expression into the most serious one he could muster. The position of Superior Court Judge is an elected one in Santa Barbara County, and representatives of every local news station and paper (not to mention the nationals) were there.

Usually a second string arraignment attorney would sit through this case, along with a stack of other arraignment matters of varying degrees on the court's calendar; but this case was so special that the District Attorney himself (and Brent's old classmate, Bradley Chernow) would be trying the case for the People, and he would start at the arraignment.

Chernow would be a formidable opponent. Not only was he smart, but he also carried the sword of the People of the State of California on his belt like a Roman soldier. That probably came from his ex-cop background. Unlike Brent, he had spent his law school days working as a policeman during the day and going to classes at night. Chernow came off, at first, as "a nice guy," but those friendly amber eyes hid the dedicated public servant that was behind them, whose only purpose in life at this particular time was to nail one crazy serial killer: Joshua Banks.

Uncle Burt greeted Brent and Bradley Chernow and read the rights of the defendant himself (instead of playing the taped version, so he would look good for the voters), and then came to the ten million dollar question to which he already knew the answer.

"Well now, Mr. Banks, you have been charged with the murder in the first degree of Ronald Bennett and James Bennett. To that charge, sir, how do you plea?" Uncle Burt put on his best serious expression. He looked a lot like Charlie Brown from Peanuts.

"I have been the prisoner of a demon, Judge! A most vile creature!"

"Mr. Banks, the only available pleas to you are 'guilty' or 'not guilty.' Mr. Marks, please advise your client."

Brent whispered to Banks. "Just say *not guilty*," and Banks nodded.

"As God is my witness, Judge, I am not guilty."

"Okay, fine."

Uncle Burt set the matter for preliminary hearing and went into recess to clear the decks for the regular day's business. Banks was taken back to his holding cell by several bailiffs and the gallery unloaded like a church on Sunday after a too-long sermon. Brent avoided talking to the press, but Chernow was only too happy to oblige all questions.

A young woman reporter from the ABC news affiliate ran after Brent and stuck her microphone in his face.

"Mr. Marks, how do you respond to the State Bar complaint made against you for unethical conduct?"

*What? What complaint?* Brent must have looked like the proverbial deer in the headlights, because she felt the need to explain her question.

"The complaint filed by Susan Fredericks, the victim's sister, that you have a conflict of interest in representing Joshua Banks."

"No comment."

Chernow heard the question and volunteered his own answer. "The District Attorney's office is looking into these allegations and has the option to file a motion to recuse Mr. Marks if we determine they are well founded."

*Thanks, Brad. I knew I could count on you.*

***

Brent received his discovery package from the District Attorney's office. The blood on Banks' shirt and pants matched the DNA of both Ronald and James Bennett. *No surprise there.* The murder weapon or weapons were never found. The task force was continuing to gather evidence against Banks to pin the other murders on him. They were sure they had found their maniac.

"Brent, Doctor Orozco on one."

"Thanks, Mims. Hello, Doc."

"Brent, I've got the tox report back on Banks. He was loaded with PCP."

"PCP?"

"Does Banks have a history of drug abuse?"

"No."

"Alright. I'll fax the report over to your office.

"Thanks, Doc."

In going over the discovery package, so many things didn't add up to Brent - and now, PCP. *Who was driving the truck that hit the jail bus? And why doesn't Salas's description of the stalker fit Banks?*

\*\*\*

"Brent, the D.A. has made his decision and that's that. We've got our guy."

Brent couldn't believe Angela could let a possibly innocent man go to prison, or perhaps lose his life. She was as convinced as Tomassi that they had their man.

"You know, Brent, that every case is like a puzzle within a puzzle within another puzzle. Some pieces are always missing, and some never would fit no matter what. We call that police work."

"We call it *reasonable doubt*."

# CHAPTER TWENTY FOUR

Brent had spent the weeks leading up to the trial going over the evidence that had been produced to him by the D.A., while Jack tried to take up where the task force had stopped investigating and started turning their investigation into a witch hunt against Joshua Banks. Once Banks had been captured wearing clothes covered with the blood of the first two victims, they had stopped pursuing all other leads and focused only on the evidence that would nail their man.

The only good thing about that was that Angela had gone back to her regular assignment. She would be called as a witness at the trial, but was no longer on the "hanging crew" with Tomassi. The case was considered solved and had turned into getting all the ducks in a row for the next murder case against Banks.

***

Roland Tomassi had reluctantly accepted a meeting with Jack Ruder, but he didn't expect it to include Brent Marks. When they stepped into Tomassi's office and sat down in front of his desk, he was on the phone. Tomassi finished up his call, put down the receiver, and looked at them with disgust.

"What's he doing here?"

"Technically, he's my boss, Rolly."

"It's bad enough that you've crossed over. Now you've got to involve the defense lawyer. And the same one who screwed our case."

Tomassi looked indignantly at Brent.

"I screwed your case?"

"You heard me. Out there playing detective, interfering with police business."

"What about the truck? What about the driver? Who's following up on those leads?"

"I can't disclose details of an ongoing investigation. You know that."

"You can when it's relevant to my client's defense."

"You talk that over with Chernow, okay? Are we done here, Jack?"

Brent wouldn't let it go. "I'll tell you why you've given up on this investigation. It's because you're sure you've got your guy."

"Of course we have our guy. There haven't been any murders since he's been back in jail."

"Oh, that certainly is proof beyond a reasonable doubt."

"And we're going to fry him. He's a walking dead man, Marks."

"And who was driving the truck? A ghost? Remote control?"

Tomassi didn't answer. He just pointed to the door with his head and then went back to his files.

"How did he escape from his shackles in the bus and kill all the deputies and prisoners? Magic?"

Jack took Brent by the elbow and ushered him out of the office. "Well, I thought that went well."

"It's up to us now, Jack.  We have to solve this case for them."

"And if we can't?"

"Then Joshua Banks will be one step closer to God, and a lot sooner than he thought."

# CHAPTER TWENTY FIVE

Jack canvassed every business in a three mile radius of the bus crash, but couldn't identify any witnesses. He covered every truck repair shop from Santa Barbara to the San Fernando Valley. Nobody had seen a large truck with the type of damage that would have been suffered hitting the bus. *Something that big just couldn't have disappeared.*

He checked the junkyards to see if any big rig had been junked lately. Another dead end, and he was at the end of his resources. Time to call in a favor. He took out his cell phone and called an old friend.

"Hey, Babs, what's up?"

"Jack?"

"One and the same."

"Jack, I haven't heard from you in ages." A pause, then: "That means you want something."

"Come on, Babs, can't I call an old friend?"

"Who you callin' old? What do you want, Jack?"

"Can you take a little peek into NCIC for me?"

"Hell, no! I could get fired for that. Or maybe worse."

"I wouldn't ask if it wasn't important. I'm at a dead end here."

"Hypothetically speaking, Jack – and this is only hypothetical – if you had access to NCIC, what would you be looking for?"

"A stolen vehicle. From the Santa Barbara area. About two months ago."

"I'll see what I can do. But whatever you do, you can't use it officially."

"I'll just use it to give me a boost; it won't get back to you or the Bureau."

\*\*\*

Jack's meeting with Tomassi went so well that he decided to follow it up with a meeting with Salas. For that, he called her and arranged to see her away from her office. The Fess Parker Resort on Cabrillo Blvd. had a great view of the beach and the Santa Barbara Pier, but it was also a quiet place to catch a drink in "unofficial circles." Jack smiled as he walked into the lounge and saw Salas sitting there, waiting for him.

"What are you grinning about?"

Jack sat down next to Salas. "I'm just happy to see you."

"Let's get one thing straight, Jack. The only reason I agreed to see you is because you were a really good cop, and I'm not feeling good about the way this investigation went down."

"In what way?"

Salas looked around, like she was paranoid.

"They could have my badge for this. I'm not going to repeat any of what I'm telling you now. It's just conjecture on my part."

Jack motioned with his hands. "What gives?"

"This is strictly off the record."

187

"Agreed: off the record."

"I'm not happy with the loose ends of the investigation."

"Me neither."

"But you have an ulterior motive. You want to get your guy off. I think he's guilty as hell."

"I want to get to the truth. Getting him off is Brent's business."

"Fair enough."

"What loose ends?"

"The truck, for one thing. Banks was inside the bus when the truck hit. Either it's a hit and run, or…"

"Or Banks isn't your guy."

"Or he has a partner. And he's still out there somewhere."

"What can you tell me on the record?"

"What I told the D.A. It's got to be in your discovery package."

"Black and white letters. It says that the guy who attacked you was about six-foot-six. Banks is five-foot eight. Tell me how you told it."

"I don't think the guy who attacked me could have been Joshua Banks."

# CHAPTER TWENTY SIX

The preliminary hearing was more like an inquisition. It was a joke really – one of the old vestiges of due process – something that Brent felt had become more of a concept than a reality in American law these days. In fact, the legal system had probably been more just under the Magna Carta than it was now. The present justice system had not much to do with anything that the so-called Founding Fathers had in mind when they broke the colonies off from the Motherland; especially in federal court, where the prosecutor has all the power and less than 3% of cases go to jury trial.

As a result, many an innocent defendant had pleaded guilty in a plea bargain – an offer they couldn't refuse.  Once a person was accused of a crime, unless he could afford a very high bail, he could look forward to spending all the time in jail that it would take to resolve his case.  A defense lawyer had little time to prepare for the case and discuss it with his client, unlike the prosecutor, who had at his disposal a battery of expert criminologists and technicians.  And he usually held over the defendant's head a higher punishment if he went to trial and lost than if he would have taken the deal.  *I'll take what's behind door number three* did not work too well in the modern justice system, which was all system and no justice.

But everything was different in Joshua Banks' case.  Everyone except for Brent, who had already decided that he was a serial killer; and Brent's vote (which was still undecided) didn't count.  *Plead guilty and throw yourself on the mercy of the court* was the offer Bradley Chernow had made.  This would be the fight of Joshua Banks' life, for his life.

# CHAPTER TWENTY SEVEN

Jack raised his eyebrows and leaned in to Salas.

"The guy who attacked me had super strength. Like a body builder or something. I kneed him square in the balls at full force and it didn't even faze him."

"You're not going to dummy up in court and say that you have no independent recollection of anything but what's in the police report, are you?"

"Jack, it's my opinion. And, even if it wasn't, it's a completely different case."

Jack frowned. "It wasn't a different case before you guys zeroed in on Joshua Banks."

Jack's cell phone rang, and he reached for it. "Excuse me a second. Jack Ruder…"

"Jack, it's Babs. I've got something for you. Can you meet me tonight?"

"Sure: where at?"

"How about the bar at Chateau Marmont?"

"What time?"

"After work. Around six-thirty?"

"See you there."

\*\*\*

Brent had arranged to get back into the Bennett home to survey the scene of the crime; something he had been planning to do when Banks had escaped custody. When he pulled up to the cottage, Susan Fredericks was there waiting, her arms crossed defensively.

"Hello, Susan."

"Brent." Her one word greeting was cold and calculated.

"So you still think your little angel is innocent?"

"Susan, I can't discuss the case with you. I just need to get in to see the house."

Susan stepped aside and made a sweeping motion toward the open door, facetiously. Brent ignored her and walked on past.

"Thank you."

Brent started in the living room. The stained carpet had been removed and the lettering painted over, but Brent just needed a lay of the land. *They're probably selling the house.* He pulled out the photographs to remind him of the positions of the bodies. As he imagined them there, he looked out the picturesque window.

"This was my brother's dream home."

"I know."

Brent felt bad for Susan, but it had nothing to do with his job. Whether Banks was guilty or not, he had to defend him. And, if he wasn't guilty, Jack was hot on the trail of whoever was.

Brent walked the corridor, imagining the blood trail from the pictures. Then he got to the bedroom.

*The killer crept up on Ron and James while they were sleeping; both nude. First he thrust his blade into James's chest, letting Ron watch in horror for a couple of seconds. Ron tried to get off the bed to run, but the killer stabbed him in the back, bringing him down in front of the bed, then stabbed him in the chest and stomach. Then he went back to James and finished him off, if he wasn't already. Finally, in a violent rage, he stabbed each already-dead body multiple times. Then he dragged first Ron, then James, down the hallway and arranged them in the quasi-sexual position. His signature was the writing on the wall in the victims' own blood.*

When Brent exited the bedroom, Susan was there.

"Are you finished?"

"Yes, Susan. I can't discuss the case with you, but I can assure you that I firmly believe that justice will be done."

# CHAPTER TWENTY EIGHT

The Santa Barbara Courthouse had a beauty that didn't seem to fit with the work that went on inside of it. It looked more like an art museum than a courthouse. But, still, the old building held the soul of every lawyer who ever had the good fortune to make a legal argument between its adobe walls. For that reason, Brent both adored and respected it. Brent had made a motion for a change of venue on the grounds that the jury pool had been tainted by the numerous stories of the case in the media. But there was no community in the state, or even the nation, that had not been inundated by stories of the Honeymoon Stalker; so the motion had been denied.

Judge Melinda Carlyle ran an efficient courtroom. Married to a star player in the D.A.'s office, she was, herself, an ex- Assistant District Attorney who had been appointed to the post by Governor Schwarzenegger (aka "The Governator.") She was quite attractive and feminine until she put the black robe on. A mother of two small children, Judge Carlyle had decided to leave her maternal instinct and her femininity at home. Her courtroom was a place for tough decisions and she had to look and act the part.

Before the process of selecting a jury, Chernow had made several motions in limine, to exclude certain evidence. One of the motions was to exclude any evidence of the other Honeymoon Stalker crimes being investigated.

A motion in limine is used to suppress or limit evidence on a particular issue or issues. If granted, it essentially blocks a party's right to present the evidence to the jury.

Chernow's motion sought to preclude the mention of any evidence uncovered in any investigation that was previously considered related to the Bennet case, but not yet solved. In other words: he was trying to prevent Brent from presenting any defenses.

Judge Carlyle called the court to order and got straight to business.

"Gentlemen, I have reviewed the People's motion and the opposition. Please don't cover anything in your argument that I have already read."

*I hope she really read them. There's nothing else to talk about.*

Chernow went ahead and touched on all the points in his motion anyway and Carlyle politely listened. She didn't want to appear disinterested in front of a crowd of reporters and potential voters.

"Your Honor, the People believe the defense will seek to poke holes in our case by introducing alleged inconsistencies between this case and other, as yet unsolved, murder investigations."

*Damn right I do.*

"These other murders have not been fully investigated and it would be highly prejudicial to the People's case if the defense were to be allowed to argue the differences between them and the case at hand."

Brent stood up. "Your Honor, Sheriff Thomas stood in front of a national audience and proclaimed that he had caught the Honeymoon

Stalker.  Never mind that my client voluntarily turned himself in.  Now the State wants to keep to itself all the evidence that makes the crimes similar and related so they can prosecute my client for the other murders, yet exclude the evidence that is inconsistent.  We cannot try each of these cases in a vacuum, Your Honor.  They are either related or they are not."

Judge Carlyle took a deep breath.  She knew this case could make the difference between a long or short judicial career.  And she knew that every ruling she made would be looked at critically; not just by the Court of Appeal, but the media and public as well.

"The court recognizes that this is a capital case.  Therefore, I'm going to give the defense leeway to present any evidence it can establish as relevant and connected to this case, on a case by case basis."

\*\*\*

The Chateau Marmont was a bit of living Hollywood History.  Set back on Sunset Boulevard near Crescent Heights, it had seen its share of celebrities and had become a celebrity itself.  When Jack walked in, he saw Babs sitting back on one of the padded benches in the classically tailored room.  Babs was Barbara

Taylor, Jack's ex-colleague from his days at the Bureau in Los Angeles and one of the ones who never faulted him for crossing over to the "dark side" of defense work. He slid in next to her and gave her a peck on the cheek.

"Hey, Babs, you look as great as ever!"

Barbara blushed and smiled a set of perfectly whitened teeth. It looked like she had even made up her turquoise eyes and put lipstick on her ample lips for the occasion. Babs was a little on the heavy side, but not hard to look at. Nothing had ever happened between them. Jack was always too much business for any monkey business.

"You're looking pretty good yourself, Jack. Next time try to call me when you don't need something. Just to talk."

Jack looked down. "I didn't want to cause you any trouble. You know, since I started working for the *other side*."

Babs smiled and stirred her drink nervously. "What are you having?"

"What's that?"

"Singapore Sling."

Jack motioned for the waiter. "I'll have a Corona."

"Yes, sir."

After the small talk was out of the way, the meeting lost its social appeal.

"So, what did you find out?"

"There's an outfit called J.C. Riley and Sons Towing in Goleta that reported one of their heavy duty wreckers was stolen, that fits within your time frame."

"Heavy duty wreckers?"

"Yeah. You know: those big tow trucks. This one can handle as much as 75 tons. It would have made toast out of that bus with minimal damage to itself."

"Was it recovered?"

"Found it down in Ventura somewhere. Sorry, Jack, but I couldn't get the report for you."

"That's okay. You did enough. I'll go over to J.C. Riley and Sons to pay them a visit."

"You didn't hear anything from me."

"No worries, Babs: that goes without saying."

# CHAPTER TWENTY NINE

Voir dire was the first process in every trial – the selection of a jury. It means "to tell the truth" in French, but it is really a process of weeding out potential jurors that each side doesn't want, and in doing so, attempts to stack the deck as much as possible in your favor against the other side without knowing anything about the prospective jurors except the way they answer the questions and the way they appear - which is probably more important.

Brent (and Chernow) each had 20 peremptory challenges which allowed him to kick potential jurors off the panel without giving a reason, and there were certain people he could *not* have on the jury: people who had relatives who had been a victim of murder and people who, themselves, (or someone close to them) had been victims of a violent crime. There was no way they could be fair and impartial, especially in this case.

But no matter how skillful Brent was in selecting a jury, the end result was still going to be a random group of individuals who each had only one thing in common – most of them to be there for this society-imposed indentured servitude, and Brent didn't want anyone on the jury who wanted to sit in judgment of his client. They each would be different, with varying degrees of intelligence, and would, based on their own biases, prejudices, and life experiences, decide sometime after the trial began (but certainly not before it had ended) whether Banks was guilty or not.

"All rise," the Clerk called as Judge Carlyle took the bench. With the long black robes that covered everything but her little head, she looked kind of like a Tim Burton cartoon character from "The Nightmare before Christmas," except not as scary.

Judge Carlyle sat down and, in her best "gruff" voice, greeted everyone and asked them to be seated. The gallery was full of spectators - mostly press - but it also held Susan Fredericks, who herself held nothing but contempt for Brent.

"We're here on the case of *People v. Joshua Banks*. Counsel, please state your appearances."

"Bradley Chernow for the People, Your Honor."

"Brent Marks representing the Joshua Banks, who is also present, Your Honor." *Where else could he be?*

"Gentlemen, are you ready to proceed?"

Brent and Chernow answered affirmatively in stereo.

"Good. Then we'll call in the first panel."

The panel was roughly half Caucasian and half Mexican American, with a smattering of African American thrown in. Brent didn't expect any of them to be sympathetic to an accused serial killer, so his job would be to try to throw out the ones who seemed as if they could make their minds up right away, without bothering to listen to any evidence. The Clerk called out the first twelve names at random, and they each took a seat in the jury box.

Brent's task was insurmountable, compared to the dozens upon dozens of times he had participated in the jury selection process. This time, he had a client who sat with him at the counsel table with wide, crazy eyes. Even adorned in the dark blue suit that Melinda had bought for Joshua Banks to wear for the trial, he was jittery, fidgeted around in his seat, and silently babbled to himself, and there was little Brent could do to control his behavior. He looked, well, just how you would expect a serial killer to look.

# CHAPTER THIRTY

Judge Carlyle walked the jurors through the basic questions regarding their families, backgrounds, employment history, history with the judicial system, prior jury service, and what they had already heard about the case. It was virtually impossible to find jurors who had not read or seen something about it in the media. She dismissed two potential jurors who she felt were not able to serve as impartial jurors, and two names were called at random from the panel to replace them. Then she turned the show over to the attorneys.

From that point on, Carlyle would be an evidence referee until the time came for her to instruct the jury on the law that applied to the case. The justice system, if you can call it that, makes for a very limited inquiry in a criminal trial. A trial is a game. The rules of the game are the rules of evidence. If a piece of evidence does not fit those rules, whether or not it has anything to do with the truth or justice, it does not come in. As a result, many a guilty defendant has walked free and, more unfortunately, many an innocent man has been sent to the prison or the gallows.

Both parties sought to load the jury with people who were biased toward their side. Brent's job was to look for skeptics: people who question authority. His main objective was to try to keep people on the jury who would pay attention, keep an open mind, and, above all else, like him. Chernow's job was to look for "law and order" people who paid their bills on time and never questioned the police. His objective would be to load the jury with as many "law and order" people as possible, and to use his peremptory challenges to kick off the jurors that Brent wanted on the panel. Joshua Banks' job was to sit there and not look crazy, which was probably the most difficult task of all.

Chernow was allowed first crack at the jurors, and chose that opportunity to give a speech about circumstantial evidence. He knew that Brent would be hitting hard on the fact that the People's case was entirely built upon circumstantial evidence, and that there was no direct evidence or eyewitness testimony that linked Banks to the crime. The fact of the matter is that most prosecutors' cases are built almost entirely upon circumstantial evidence, and a good set of circumstantial facts is just as good as direct evidence to hang a guilty verdict on. It didn't take Chernow long to learn that most of the panel had no problem with the concept, and he noted the ones who hesitated. They wouldn't be spending any more time in the jury box.

Next, he talked about the death penalty. Nobody had been executed in California for years because its death penalty had been shot down by several court rulings, but that didn't stop the young D.A. from seeking to fry Joshua Banks. He just wanted to make sure everyone sitting in that box had no problem with it. Everyone who did was dismissed with a peremptory challenge.

Chernow then went into his general questions, designed to show bias by the raise of hands. After that, he started prying into the private lives of every juror; asking everything from favorite hobbies and TV shows to how much time they spent on social media and what websites they frequented the most.

When the floor was turned over to Brent, he gave a little speech about the burden of proof and reasonable doubt. It was the People's case to prove every element of murder beyond a reasonable doubt. The defendant didn't have to do anything. Brent was there to raise the specter of reasonable doubt in everything he possibly could. The problem was that nobody really understood what reasonable doubt was, and that made it equally difficult to explain. That problem was coupled with the fact that, since it was not final argument, Brent couldn't tell the potential jurors what his definition of reasonable doubt was: he was therefore stuck with the one in the jury instruction book.

Reasonable doubt was defined as "not ordinary doubt," which was confusing enough. It required the jurors to decide whether each essential element of the case has been proved by the People to the point of an abiding conviction in them that the charge was true. The judge would instruct them as to reasonable doubt as well as all the law they would apply to the case, and would shuffle them off to the jury room to decide the fate of Joshua Banks by the seats of their pants.

When the dust had finally cleared on voir dire, there remained five Mexican American men, three Mexican American women, one African American man, two Caucasian men and one woman, and two white male alternates whose job would be to sit through the whole trial, take notes, and not end up participating in decision making unless another juror took sick or was incapacitated.

"The People accept the jury as presently constituted, Your Honor."

The easy part was over.

# CHAPTER THIRTY ONE

J.C. Riley and Sons Towing was one of the largest towing companies in Santa Barbara County. It had a huge inventory of trucks of all different types and a large staff of drivers. Jack met with Tom Riley, one of the "sons," at their main office on Hollister Avenue. Riley was a big man who had not yet seen fifty, with huge biceps that had faded motorcycle tattoos on them. One of the biceps held a pack of cigarettes rolled up in the sleeve of his short-sleeved shirt. *Looks like he saw the light and joined his father's business before it was too late.*

Riley greeted Jack with a death grip handshake as he made direct eye contact.

"You a cop?"

"Ex-cop. I'm a private investigator now. I'm working on the Honeymoon Stalker case."

"The bad guys?"

"Our guy got a bum rap. You can understand that, can't you?"

"Yeah, I guess. But I already talked to the cops."

"You got the truck back?"

"Yeah, and they already went over it and released it. It's already been fixed."

"Mind if I see it?"

"Sure."

Riley led Jack through the yard, full of tow trucks and grease monkeys, to a line of heavy duty tow trucks four deep. The one he pointed out was a monster, with several axles and 18 wheels.

"Here she is." Riley put his hand on the brand new front end.

"Was she damaged badly?"

"Took a couple a dents, but she was still runnin."

"Where'd they find her?"

"Down by the beach in Ventura. The cops have all that."

"You got video surveillance on the yard?"

"Yeah."

"How far does it go back?"

"Bout six months."

"Can I see it?"

"Sure, come on in the office."

Riley's office was at the end of the yard. It had several secretaries, an accountant and a security guard at a security station, and was equipped with video monitors of the yard. Riley pulled up two plastic chairs for himself and Jack at the security station. He withdrew his pack of cigarettes from his sleeve, slapped the pack against his palm several times, opened it, and pulled out a cigarette with his mouth.

"The date we're looking at is May $14^{th}$."

"Bertha was reported missing on the $14^{th}$." Riley flicked his lighter, lit his cigarette and drew in a deep hit.

"Can you play the video from the $13^{th}$?"

Riley blew out smoke and sped through the video.

"Wait, stop there."

Riley rewound the video.

"Bertha's not there."

"No, she's not." Riley's words appeared with puffs of smoke.

"Can you rewind it some more? I'll tell you where to stop."

Riley rolled back the video until they could see Bertha in her place.

"Stop. Could you play it back now?"

The video showed a figure, dressed in black, getting into Bertha and driving it away.

"Can you freeze it there? Yeah, there. Thanks."

It was impossible to identify any facial features. The figure had his back to the camera at all times. It's like he knew exactly where it was.

"Could I get a copy of that footage?"

"Sure."

"Mr. Riley, do you know if Bertha was hot wired or if the thief used a key?"

"Looked to me like he used a key."

"Do you have any employees who are overly religious?"

"Ain't no sin to be a good Christian."

"I'm not talking about Christians or normal people who are religious. I'm talking about a real nut. Someone who talks about demons and Satan and God all the time."

Riley's eyes widened. "You're talkin' about Dusty."

"Dusty?"

"Dusty Clairborne." He pulled out another cigarette and put it in his mouth. It flapped around as he spoke. "One of our drivers. You think he stole Bertha?"

"Maybe. Maybe even more than that. Can I talk to Dusty?"

"Nope." Riley lit up again, blowing out smoke.

"Why not?"

"Dusty quit about a month ago."

# CHAPTER THIRTY TWO

Bradley Chernow took the stage first, at the lectern that had been set in front of the jury box, with an opening statement that made even Brent ashamed to be sitting next to Joshua Banks, acting as his lawyer. *Bad guys need lawyers too. Especially bad guys.* The opening statement, not surprisingly, concentrated on the pure evil of the act.

"And, in a fury of rage, ladies and gentlemen, this man, Joshua Banks..." Chernow pointed an accusatory finger at Banks. "This man crept into the bedroom of Ronald and James Bennett, and stabbed them both to death..."

"No, no, it wasn't me! It was the demon!" Banks leapt up in his chair at counsel table."

"Your Honor!"

"It was the demon! A most evil creature, sent to earth by the Devil himself! He did these things!"

Brent yanked on Banks' jacket and pulled him back into his seat. Brent caught a glimpse of both courtroom deputies, on alert, with their hands on their guns and hoped that the jury had not seen them as well. Banks was competent to stand trial in the eyes of the law, but he was incompetent to defend himself.

"Mr. Banks, be quiet! You're not helping your case this way."

"Mr. Marks, please control your client or I will have him restrained." Judge Carlyle cautioned Brent and admonished the jury.

"The jury will disregard the outbursts of the defendant. Mr. Chernow, you may continue."

"The evidence will show that there is indeed a demon, and he is sitting right there in this courtroom!"

Brent held himself back. It was argumentative, and strictly not allowed, but he let it go.

"The evidence will show that this man, Joshua Banks, silently crept into the bedroom of Ronald and James Bennett, *while they were sleeping*, and stabbed Ronald Bennett at least four times, and James Bennett at least four times, which was enough to kill them both. But did he stop there? No! He stabbed Ronald Bennett at least another nineteen times and James Bennett at least twenty two times more."

"No, no, no, no!" Banks whispered to himself, and rocked back and forth in his chair. There was nothing Brent could do. He whispered to Banks, "Mr. Banks, be quiet and calm down. You're making yourself look guilty."

There was a look of sheer horror on each of the juror's faces. The men grimaced with every detail, and the ladies closed their eyes. Chernow saw that his words were accomplishing just exactly what he intended, and he stepped into the well of the courtroom, away from the podium and closer to the jury.

"There was no way they could escape the fury of this evil and heinous murderer. The stab wounds in their chests and backs punctured their heart, lungs and liver. Then he dragged the bodies to their living room, posed them in a sexual position, and wrote, *in their own blood*, 'GOD HATES FAGS' on their living room wall."

"The evidence will further show, ladies and gentlemen, that the defendant, Joshua Banks, is a religious zealot who committed prior violent acts toward the victims and was vocal in his opposition to their lifestyle as a same-sex married couple."

"But it's a sin! God says it's a sin, punishable by death," Banks mumbled. "Thou shalt not lay with a man as with a woman."

"Banks, shut up!"

The men on the jury had turned their attention from Chernow and were now staring at Banks. *It's a lynch mob. And we're not even finished with opening statements.*

"Ladies and gentlemen, the evidence will show that there is no reasonable doubt that this was a hate motivated crime, calculated with premeditation and malice, and that the defendant, Joshua Banks, is guilty of the first degree multiple murders of James and Ronald Bennett."

"Thank you, Mr. Chernow. The Court will now recess for lunch. When we recommence at 1:30, we will have the opening statement of the defendant."

Brent and Chernow stood up to pay respect for the jury as they filed out. They would now try to eat their ham and cheese sandwiches and

222

hamburgers with the horrific images that Chernow had implanted in their brains. Brent jerked Banks to his feet. After they had left, the judge turned her view from the departing jury to Brent. Then, the judge motioned to the bailiffs to take Banks into custody.

"Counsel, approach the bench."

Brent slinked up to the judge's altar like a guilty dog who had stolen a sausage. Chernow was trying to suppress his glee. The judge looked sternly at Brent.

"Mr. Marks. Your client has a right to be present during these proceedings. I don't want to have him shackled to counsel table with a guard watching him, but I will do it if it is necessary to keep order in my courtroom."

"Yes, Your Honor."

"So, do your best to control your client or I will have to take extreme measures to do so."

"Yes, Your Honor."

*The jury's ready to vote right now.* Brent put on his best face of self-confidence as he left the bench. It seemed impossible to clean the stain that had just been cast upon Joshua Banks.

# CHAPTER THIRTY THREE

Brent felt like Custer must have felt during his last stand, and the trial had only just begun. The first things the jurors heard and the last things they would hear as jurors were the details of the horrific murders, and now, with those images of the bloody hate crime indelibly etched in their hearts and souls, he was going to talk to them about ethereal concepts, like reasonable doubt and circumstantial evidence. The idea that this gay-hating heathen to whom they had just been introduced (and who acted the part in court) was entitled to a presumption that he was innocent until proven guilty would be challenging.

These vague concepts which the members of the jury would probably hear for the very first time could not possibly compete for their attention like the visceral images that had been painted by Chernow in his opening statement. Those images had  percolated in their respective brains during the 1 ½ hour lunch break and, as the jury took their seats at 1:30, they were all looking at Banks. *I say we hang 'im, and then we kill 'im.*

Brent approached the jury like the last standing Native American at Wounded Knee.  To do that, he embarked on educating them about a fiction in the law that every person accused of a crime was innocent until proven guilty.  He knew full well that the contrary was true.  His client had been branded and tattooed, and now it was up to him to change their perspective.  *Good luck. Here goes…*

"Ladies and gentlemen, good afternoon. We've all heard the gory details of this most atrocious murder.  As an officer of the court and a fellow human being who personally knew both of the victims, I have nothing but respect for their lives and mourn their deaths, along with all of their family and friends."

Brent glanced out of the corner of his eye at Susan Fredericks, who was scowling.

"The evidence will surely show just how violent, horrific, pointless and terrible these murders were.     But, your job as jurors is to listen to *all* the evidence and, based upon the law that will be given to you by the judge, decide if the prosecutor has proven every element of the crime against my client, Joshua Banks."

"As terrible as the murders were, the law requires that you treat Joshua as presumed innocent.   We lawyers often use the phrase, "cloaked in innocence" to describe this. Imagine, if you will, that Joshua is covered in a blanket of innocence.   Joshua does not have to do anything to prove or disprove *anything*. He doesn't have to *say* anything.   The prosecution *alone* has the burden to convince each and every one of you that he has proven every element of the crime beyond a reasonable doubt, to an abiding conviction."

*They're listening, but already they don't trust me.*

"If Mr. Chernow does not satisfy his burden to prove every element beyond a reasonable doubt, you must acquit Joshua.  Why is this so important?  Because the case against Joshua is based entirely upon circumstantial evidence. You won't hear from any witness who actually saw who committed these murders. Circumstantial evidence can be very, very dangerous.  I'll give you an example.

"I once had a client who was accused of molesting his one-year-old daughter. He was arrested and tried on the basis of one statement, *Papa did it.* In the trial it was revealed that "Papa" was the name she called her grandfather. The judge will instruct you that, if the circumstantial evidence leads you to two inferences, one of which points to Joshua's innocence, and one of which points to his guilt, you *must* choose the inference that points to his innocence.

Brent paused and regarded the jury to see if anything had sunk in. They still looked somber. *I hope they're so serious because they're intently listening.*

"You must look at every element of this crime through the looking glass of reasonable doubt. The judge will instruct you that reasonable doubt is more than mere doubt. It is when you lack an abiding conviction as to whether some element of the crime has been proven or not.

"What does this mean in life? We've all experienced reasonable doubt. It's the doubt you have that makes you want to double check. It's what makes you question, "Did I turn off the iron?" when you leave the house. Nine times out of ten, you did. But there's that one time... It's what makes you reach into your jacket pocket

228

before you leave to make sure you have the concert tickets.

"We believe the evidence will show questions of reasonable doubt. For example, the People will present evidence that a huge truck crashed into the jail bus as it transported my client from the courthouse to the jail, and that my client escaped police custody. The prosecutor will ask you to draw an inference that my client was guilty because of his flight. However, there are pieces to this puzzle that are missing which should raise the specter of reasonable doubt in your minds. The truck left the scene. Who was driving the truck when it hit the bus? The People will present Detective Rhonda Salas, who had a confrontation with the so-called "Honeymoon Stalker.""

"Objection. Irrelevant, Your Honor. That is a different case."

"Counsel approach."

Brent argued that the prosecution couldn't have it both ways. Chernow couldn't introduce evidence of Banks' flight and then not allow Brent to raise inferences that led away from Banks as the perpetrator. And since Banks was a suspect in all the cases, Chernow couldn't prevent Brent from introducing evidence of the differences between Banks' physical makeup and the description given by Salas of the perpetrator. The judge agreed and Brent and Chernow took back their fighting positions.

"As I was saying, the prosecutor will present Detective Rhonda Salas, who had a confrontation with the so-called Honeymoon Stalker. But she will give a physical description of a man who is a much taller than Joshua Banks.

"Ladies and gentlemen, the prosecution will say that my client is guilty, but the police have no claim to the absolute truth than anyone else. All the defense asks of you is to weigh each element of this crime on the scales of reasonable doubt. Thank you."

Brent could see the recognition in every juror. The wheels of their minds were churning. *If only ten percent of what I've said sinks in, maybe at least a few of you will think.*

# CHAPTER THIRTY FOUR

He crouched in the darkness and prayed. *Our Father, who art in Heaven, hallowed be thy name.* He needed guidance; something from the spirit. He was confused and disoriented and, for the first time, was not hearing clearly the voice he had heard before: the voice from Heaven of the Lord Himself. He prayed for that connection to be re-established. *Lord, have I failed you? Is this a test of some kind?*

His mind drifted back to the killings. Yes, they had to be done; it was his duty. But still, there was something that bothered him about them. It was the way he felt. How he had enjoyed spilling the blood of the infidels. Relished the shrieking sounds of their deaths. *Oh, Lord, show me the light! Wash me of my sinful feelings!* Then his head fell like a doll with a broken neck, and he cried.

***

Jack took a night meeting with Brent at Sonny's Bar and Grill on State Street. The music was loud, but they had a quiet corner where they always conducted business over a brew. When Brent met up with Jack, he looked very somber.

"What's up, Jack?"

"Chernow's holding out on you, that's what."

Jack told Brent about his meeting with Riley, that the police had a copy of the stolen vehicle report on Bertha, and had interviewed Riley and taken a copy of the surveillance video. He turned over the video and his report to Brent.

"But the buck stopped there. They never followed up on Dusty Clairborne as a suspect."

"Because they don't care. They have Banks and they've got their blinders on. It's up to you to solve their case for them, Jack. "

"And Chernow?"

"I'll deal with him."

***

When court convened the next morning, Brent took Chernow aside.

"Can I talk to you a second?"

"Sure, what's on your mind?"

"You've been holding back discovery on me."

"I resent that."

"Whatever. My investigator just uncovered the stolen vehicle report on the tow truck that smashed into the bus, the security video, and identified a suspect. My discovery package has none of that. I want all of it, Brad, and I want it now or I'm going to move for a mistrial."

"That's confidential information on a pending investigation."

"Bullshit. It's information that reasonably leads to admissible evidence in this case and I'm entitled to it. What else are you not telling me, Brad? Do I have to make a motion before the judge for all the discovery I'm supposed to get? Do you really want a mistrial in this case?"

Chernow frowned. "I'll make sure you have an updated package by noon."

"And you'll stipulate that I be allowed to recall your investigators on cross or as part of my case-in-chief?"

"Yes."

"Thank you."

\*\*\*

"You're holding out on us, Rolly."

Jack leaned across Detective Tomassi's desk and looked him straight in the eye.

"I don't know what you're talking about."

"The stolen tow truck. Dusty Clairborne?"

Tomassi was indignant. "First of all, Jack, I can't comment on an active investigation. Second of all, the truck was clean. No fingerprints, no trace evidence. Nothing to connect it to the murders. A hit and run, plain and simple."

"Did you talk to Clairborne?"

"What for? It's a hit and run. I referred it to the appropriate department. Detectives determined it was a hit and run. Clairborne was cleared."

"So Banks just got out of his handcuffs and restraints like Harry Houdini and killed everyone on the bus?"

"This isn't show and tell, Jack. You'll have to wait for court for that."

"You've narrowed your investigation. Once you had the bloody clothes on Banks, you stopped following all other leads. Maybe even before then."

Tomassi's cheeks tightened. He clenched his fists. "Look, Mr. FBI-turned-rogue. I don't need you questioning my investigation. He escaped and there were more murders. Then, he shows up high as a fucking kite in clothes soaked in the victim's blood. Now, if you'll excuse me, I've got work to do."

"What about the inconsistencies?"

"There're always things that don't fit in an investigation. Your guy did it, and that's that. "

Jack got up and turned to leave. He turned back. "Exactly my point."

# CHAPTER THIRTY FIVE

It was no surprise to Brent that Chernow called Susan Fredericks as his first witness. She would paint a picture of the murders that would forever dwell in the minds of each juror. More importantly, it would switch on their emotional brains and throw logic out the window. It was through her emotional testimony that Chernow would seek to admit the most repulsive photographs of the murder scene. Better her than the investigators, who were not personally involved.

A teary-eyed Susan Fredericks took the stand and described the day she discovered her brother's murder.

"Ms. Fredericks, can you please describe your relationship to the victims?"

"James Fredericks Bennett was my brother, and Ronald Bennett was my brother-in-law."

"The victims had just been recently married before the murders?"

"Yes."

"Now, Ms. Fredericks, I don't want to belabor the obvious, but James and Ronald Bennett were a gay couple, isn't that correct?"

"Yes, they were."

"And you were the person who discovered their bodies, is that correct?"

"Yes." Susan wiped a tear from her eye and reached for the Kleenex box on the witness stand.

"Ms. Fredericks, I know that this is difficult for you, so if you need to stop at any time and take a break, let me know."

"Okay."

It was theatrical, but Brent couldn't object. That would make him look like a jerk, and it was important that the jury like him. Nice guys may finish last, but in a courtroom they are king.

"Ms. Fredericks, please describe what you observed on May second of this year when you visited your brother's home."

Susan Fredericks knocked the ball out of the park for Chernow with genuine, heartfelt testimony of her gruesome discovery.

"When I entered the living room, the first thing I saw was writing on the wall, in blood."

Brent could have objected to Susan's lack of knowledge of the fact that it was blood, but it was coming out in the evidence anyway, so he let it go. The less he appeared to hassle this witness, the better.

"What did it say?"

Susan buried her face in her hands and cried. She looked up, tears streaming down her cheeks.

"It said *GOD HATES FAGS.*"

"What did you observe next?"

"I saw their bodies on the living room floor, covered with blood. They were posed in a 69 position."

Again, Brent could have objected to the sexual connotation, but it was patently obvious.

"It was so horrible, I had to get out of there right away!"

"So the only rooms you went into were the foyer and the living room."

"Yes."

"Ms. Fredericks, I'm showing you a photograph that has been marked as People's Exhibit 1."

Chernow placed a photograph of her dead brother and his husband on the witness stand. Susan took one look at it and looked away, then wailed, and covered her mouth and nose with Kleenex. Chernow deliberately paused for full effect. Brent kept his eyes on Susan, empathetically, but, with his peripheral vision, he checked the jurors. Every one of them was with her. The women were wiping tears from their own eyes.

"I'm sorry to put you through this, Ms. Fredericks, but can you please identify the people in this photograph?"

She looked at the photograph quickly, then looked away.

"It's my brother and his husband."

"And does it correctly depict the way you found them on May second?"

"Yes."

"Your Honor, I move Exhibit 1 into evidence."

"Any objection?"

"No, Your Honor."

"It is received."

Chernow placed another photograph on the witness stand. "I'm showing you another photograph marked as People's Exhibit number 2 and ask you if you can identify it."

"Yes, this is the message that I found on the living room wall."

"Again, does it correctly depict the living room wall the way you saw it on May the second?"

"Yes, it does."

Chernow milked Susan's testimony for all it was worth, then handed over the broken, emotionally spent witness to Brent for cross-examination.

"Mr. Marks? Cross-examination?"

"No questions at this time, Your Honor."

Questioning Susan Fredericks would have been an act of judicial suicide.

# CHAPTER THIRTY SIX

Detective Roland Tomassi was Chernow's next witness. He would outline the murders and point all inferences toward Joshua Banks for the jury: that would act as the master plan for the prosecution's case. Tomassi testified that he was the first officer on the scene and described what he saw, allowing Chernow to introduce even more horrific photographs of the bodies. He described the blood-stained corridor and bedroom death site, which paved the way for Chernow's blood spatter expert. Tomassi testified that the site had been secured, not contaminated, and that every piece of evidence had been accounted for. He testified as to the stab wounds he had observed on the victims, leading the way for the Coroner's testimony. Banks sat next to Brent, listening curiously .

"Both victims had multiple stab wounds all over their chests, backs and abdominal areas."

"Detective Tomassi, after securing the scene, did you identify any persons of interest?"

"Yes.    After consulting with Detective Rhonda Salas, we determined that Joshua Banks was a person of interest in the investigation."

"What led you to that determination?"

"The defendant had threatened the victims, which led to the issuance of a restraining order against him."

"Your Honor, I have marked for identification the Restraining Order of the Superior Court as People's Exhibit 23 and ask that it be admitted into evidence."

"Objection, Mr. Marks?"

"No, Your Honor."

"It is received."

"Thank you, Your Honor.    Detective, upon determining that the defendant was a person of interest, what did you do next?"

"Since we had the restraining order, we went to the defendant's house to investigate. Upon arrival, the defendant made a spontaneous admission that made me determine that I should arrest him."

"Objection and move to strike legal characterization of 'spontaneous admission.'"

"Sustained."

It probably would have been better for Brent to let it go, but the statement would have come out anyway.

"What did he tell you?"

"In response to our question of whether he was armed with a weapon, he said, "I did it and God will forgive me."

"And was it based upon that statement that you arrested him?"

"Yes. I told him not to make any further statements until I had advised him of his rights."

Brent trained his eyes on Tomassi, and his peripherals were on the jury. Tomassi was a good witness. *You're leaving a lot of things out, but I'll get you on cross.*

"And did you then Mirandize the defendant?"

"Yes, I did."

"And you took him into custody?"

"Yes."

"What happened after you took the defendant into custody?"

"The defendant was arraigned in court. Upon being transported from his arraignment, a hit and run tow truck hit the Sheriff's bus and the defendant escaped from custody."

Tomassi described the manhunt for Banks, up to the point that he turned himself in.

"When the defendant was recaptured, he was wearing bloody clothes. We had the clothes tested and they came up positive for the DNA of both Ronald and James Bennett. It was their blood."

The jurors' mouths seemed to drop, and they hung on every word.

"Showing you what has been marked collectively as People's Exhibit number 46, can you identify these, Detective?"

"Yes, these are the bloody clothes that the defendant was wearing when we took him back into custody."

*\*\**

Jack knocked on the door of apartment 216 in the Simi Valley Flats building. He heard a muffled voice from the other side of the door.

"Who's there?"

"Detective Ruder, please open the door."

"Let me see your badge."

Jack showed his LEOSA card from the FBI, the ID which allowed him to carry a weapon as a retired agent, conveniently covering the word "retired" with his finger, and the door opened. Standing before Jack was a tower of a man in a jeans jumpsuit with a white tank top which exposed huge tattooed biceps. Jack had to look up to see his face.

"Are you Dusty Clairborne?"

"Yeah. What do you want?"

"I'd like to talk to you about your employment with J.C. Riley and Sons. May I come in?"

The man hesitated, then stepped aside.

"Sure."

Jack's observant eyes roamed all over the immediate area as the man showed him to a chair in his living room.  The walls were adorned with various crosses and prints of religious paintings. There was a large bible on the coffee table that had hundreds of paper bookmarks in it; some of which had yellowed with age.

"I see you're an art collector."

"What's this all about?"

"A vehicle was reported stolen from J.C. Riley back in May."

"Yeah.  The cops already talked to me about that.  I had nothing to do with it."

"We just wanted to know if you knew anything about it."

"What would I know?"

"There have been several violent crimes against gays recently.

"So?  What does that have to do with me?"

"Maybe nothing, sir.  Our information indicates that you don't take too kindly to gays."

"Their sinful lives are their own business."

"So you think that all gays are sinners?"

"Not me.  God."

"Do you think that gay men should be put to death?"

"I don't think it, Detective. It's in the Bible. It's God's word."

Jack knew he was pushing Clairborne's buttons, and that the man was getting agitated.

"So, was it you who killed James and Ronald Bennett?"

"Who are you talking about? Get out of my house!"

"Are you attempting to hide evidence from us, Mr. Clairborne?"

"Get out! I know my rights." Clairborne stood up, his face reddened and fists clenched. Jack rose and took his leave.

"I'll be back."

"Not without a warrant."

"Suit yourself."

Jack found a place on the street to park and observe Clairborne's apartment building. It would be a long day and night, but he had no other leads to follow. He pulled out his cell to call Brent.

"Brent, it's Jack. How's the trial going?"

"Getting killed.  How about you?"

"I might be on to something.  I'm staking out Dusty Clairborne's apartment.  I'll keep you up to date."

"No pressure, Jack.  All we need is a miracle."

# CHAPTER THIRTY SEVEN

The jurors filed into court and took their assigned seats, after having had a chance for Susan Fredericks's and Detective Tomassi's damaging testimonies to sink in. Brent would now have the opportunity to cross-examine Tomassi. With that task, he would be walking a very thin line. He needed to point out discrepancies in Tomassi's testimony which lead to reasonable doubt. In Tomassi's case, what he had left out would be more important than what he had said. Brent knew that, in every case, the police routinely either lie or leave out essential details. He had to coax these details out of Tomassi without looking like he was trying to be tricky or deceptive. Joshua Banks sat next to Brent at the counsel table. He had been given a mild sedative, so he looked a little out of it. Brent glanced at him. *Better than the alternative. At least he's quiet.* Then Brent rose and confronted Tomassi.

"Detective Tomassi, yesterday you testified about the stab wounds you observed on the victims. Isn't it true that you never found the knife that you suspected made those stab wounds?"

"Yes, that's true. We never found the knife."

"In fact, you never found any knife which could have been used to make the wounds you observed, isn't that correct?"

"That is correct."

Tomassi still wore his poker face, but Brent was just getting started.

"Detective Tomassi, you testified that when you first confronted Mr. Banks, he told you that he did it and God would forgive him. Didn't he tell you in the same conversation that he threw the stone?"

"Yes, he did."

"And when you told him he was under arrest for murder, he acted surprised, didn't he?"

"I wouldn't say that."

"You were asking him about the murder but he responded to you about throwing the stone through the window, isn't that correct?"

"He did talk about throwing the stone through the window, yes."

*Come on, just say it, man!*

"And that act of throwing the stone was the subject of the restraining order, isn't that correct?"

"Yes."

"And when you told him he was under arrest for murder, he asked who had accused him of this act, isn't that correct?"

"Yes."

"And he also asked you who the victims of the murder were?"

"Yes."

"But it's obvious, Detective, isn't it; that Mr. Banks knew the victims - isn't that correct?"

Chernow leaped from his chair. "Objection, argumentative!"

"Overruled."

"I would say so, yes."

"So, wouldn't you say, then, that when Mr. Banks told you he *did it*, this *it* he was talking about was throwing the stone through the window, not the murder?"

"Objection! Argumentative." Tomassi sat mute.

"Sustained. The jury will disregard the question."

*Too late, they've already heard it.*

"Detective Tomassi, isn't it true that Mr. Banks turned himself in to the Sheriff's Department?"

"I think you turned him in."

"But he wasn't captured, isn't that correct?"

"Yes, that is correct."

"You testified yesterday that Mr. Banks escaped from custody after a hit and run incident with the Sheriff's bus, isn't that correct?"

"Yes."

"Did you discover, through investigation, that the bus was hit by a large tow truck?"

"Yes, we did."

"And did you discover that this tow truck had been stolen?"

"Yes."

"What did you do after you discovered that the tow truck had been stolen?"

"Turned it over to the detectives in our department who handle stolen vehicles."

"Did they have a suspect named Dusty Clairborne?"

"Yes, but he checked out."

"He checked out, meaning that he was eliminated as a suspect in the tow truck theft and hit and run?"

"That's right."

"But not by you, correct?"

"Correct."

"Who is the detective in charge of that investigation?"

"Detective Maloney; but the case is closed."

"There were no latent fingerprints found on the bus, correct?"

"That's correct."

"And the suspect, Dusty Clairborne, was an employee at the towing company, J.C. Riley and Sons, isn't that correct?"

"Yes, he was."

"You never questioned the suspect, did you?"

"There was no need."

Brent moved closer to the witness stand, but not close enough to fall into the "well" - the designated "no man's land" he was not allowed to step into without court permission.

"Because you already had Mr. Banks as a suspect and were focusing only on him in the murder investigation, isn't that correct, Detective?"

"Objection! Argumentative!"

Tomassi's face turned red and he tightened his chin and clenched his teeth to restrain his anger.

"Sustained. The jury will disregard the question."

"Mr. Banks was handcuffed in the jail bus, wasn't he?"

"I don't know if he was or not."

"Detective, surely you know the procedures for transporting prisoners from court to the jail, don't you?"

"Yes."

"And one of those procedures is that the prisoners must be restrained by handcuffs, correct?"

"Yes."

"Then, there is no doubt in your mind that he was handcuffed at the time?"

"He most likely was."

"And shackled?"

"Yes."

"The shackling consists of the handcuffs and a black box covering a chain between the two handcuffs, isn't that correct?"

"Yes."

"And a chain connected to the black box went around his torso, correct?"

"Yes."

"And one of his legs was shackled to the bus, is that correct?"

"That is the procedure."

"And the bus contained three deputies from the Santa Barbara Sheriff's Department, didn't it?"

"Yes."

"And all of them were armed with handguns?"

"Yes, they were."

"Is it your opinion that Mr. Banks was able to escape his restraints of handcuffs and a black box padlocked to a body chain around his torso, and one of his legs chained to the bus, and overpower three armed deputies in order to escape?"

"Objection, Your Honor! Compound and argumentative."

"The detective is capable of expressing such an opinion, Your Honor."

"I don't have an opinion. I just know that he did it."

"You know that he did it. He's quite the Houdini, isn't he, detective?"

"Objection! Argumentative!" Chernow was red in the face.

"Sustained. The jury will disregard the question."

"Isn't it true, Detective Tomassi, that you are investigating several murders that are similar to the Bennet murders?"

"Yes."

"And a task force has been formed to investigate these murders, including the Bennet murders?"

"Yes, that is true."

"During the course of the investigation by the task force, one of the members of your team, Detective Salas, was attacked by the suspect, isn't that correct?"

"Yes."

"She was attacked in her bed while she was sleeping, by a man with a knife, isn't that correct?"

"Yes."

"And she gave a description of her attacker, didn't she?"

"Yes, she did."

"She said that her attacker was about six foot five or six, didn't she?"

"Yes."

"And very strong?"

"Yes."

"This doesn't fit the description of Joshua Banks, does it?"

"Objection, calls for speculation and a legal conclusion."

"Your Honor, this man is a trained police officer. It is certainly an observation within his expertise."

"Overruled."

"The physical description she gave varies."

"Mr. Banks is about five-eight, isn't he?"

"I'm not sure."

"Why don't you refer to your report? He's about five-eight, correct?"

Tomassi looked at his police report.

"That's what it says."

*Good, it sounds like he's being evasive.*

"Detective Tomassi, isn't it true that Detective Salas was describing a person drastically different in physical characteristics than Joshua Banks?"

"Objection: calls for speculation, opinion."

"Your Honor, this witness is qualified to express such an opinion."

"Overruled. You may answer the question."

"You'll have to ask Salas."

"I will. Move to strike as non-responsive, Your Honor."

The judge turned toward Tomassi, perturbed. "Detective, is the description of the suspect who attacked Detective Salas drastically different than Mr. Banks, or not?"

"In height. But there's an explanation for that."

"Move to strike after *in height,* Your Honor."

"Sustained. The jury will disregard everything after *in height*."

"You remember the bloody clothes that Mr. Banks was wearing when he turned himself in to the Sheriff's station, don't you, Detective?"

"Yes."

"These clothes, marked as People's Exhibit 46?"

Brent held up the clothes.

"This is an extra-large black sweatshirt and black jeans, sized 38 waist and 36 inseam, correct?"

"If you say so."

"Look in your report, Detective."

Tomassi flipped through the pages of his report impatiently, until he came to the correct section.

"Yes, that size is correct."

"Detective Tomassi, isn't it true that ever since you zeroed in on Joshua Banks as a suspect, your investigation has focused on gathering evidence against him and nobody else?"

"He is the primary suspect."

Brent turned to look at the jury, sweeping the box to make eye contact, then back to Tomassi.

"He's your *only* suspect, isn't he, detective?"

"Yes."

Brent turned to look at the jury.

"And he's always been your only suspect."

"Yes."

"No further questions, Your Honor."

Brent turned away from Tomassi, dismissing him respectfully as he took his seat at counsel table, next to the near catatonic Joshua Banks.

*That was a nice injection of reasonable doubt.*

# CHAPTER THIRTY EIGHT

Jack watched through binoculars as Dusty Clairborne carried boxes to his car. *He's on the move.* Dusty finally came out with the last load –a small tent, a sleeping bag and camping equipment. *He's going camping?* Dusty slammed his trunk, got in the car – a 70's era AMC Pacer - and fired it up. *I'd love to get a look at what's in there.* Jack set the binoculars down on the passenger's seat and started his car, preparing to follow him.

Dusty pulled out onto Los Angeles Avenue and turned left on Erringer. *He's headed for the freeway.* As the Pacer chugged up the onramp, Jack ran through his options. He whipped out his cell phone and called 9-1-1.

"9-1-1, what is your emergency?"

"This is Jack Ruder. I'm a retired FBI agent. I'm driving behind a guy on the northbound 118 who is under the influence of alcohol. I'm afraid he's going to hurt somebody."

"What is your location, sir?"

"About half a mile west of the Tapo Canyon exit. It is a Blue AMC Pacer, California license 365 Adam Tom X-ray."

"Thank you for your call, sir. We will call an officer to respond."

"Should I stay on the line?"

"No, sir. We'll take it from here."

Jack fell back so Clairborne could not see he was being tailed, and waited for the CHP to respond. *Take your time, guys. It's just a serial killer.*

Finally, when Clairborne had just passed Stearns Street, a black and white CHP unit passed Jack and fell in behind the Pacer. After following him for the next mile, the red lights went on. Jack pulled off the freeway a good distance behind to observe.

The officer approached the driver's side window, looking into the fish bowl interior of the

Pacer. The officer stood next to the window as Clairborne rolled it down.

"Hello, sir. May I have your license and registration, please?"

"What's this about, Officer?"

"We had a report that you were seen driving erratically. Have you been drinking, sir?"

"No."

"License and registration, please."

Clairborne provided his license and registration.

"Would you step out of the car please, sir?"

The officer moved back a few steps and Clairborne got out of the car. Then the officer administered several field sobriety tests.

*Come on! Come on! Search the car!*

Jack strained to see details through his binoculars. This could have been his big break, but it looked like it wasn't going to happen. The officer allowed Clairborne to get back into his car and handed his license and registration back to him.

Clairborne pulled back into the flow of traffic and Jack followed behind him.

*Time for Plan B.*

Chernow took Tomassi on redirect and succeeded in rehabilitating him in the jury's eyes.

"Detective, you testified that there was an explanation for the difference in the description of the height between the suspect Detective Salas described and that of the defendant. What is that explanation?"

"Detective Salas had only fractions of a second to observe the suspect. Her state of mind, and her primary goal was to keep from getting killed."

"And the defendant's selection of clothes sizes did not strike you as odd?"

"No."

"Why not?"

"Because those were the clothes he was actually wearing. He had them on."

The long day in court took a lot out of Brent, but he wasn't looking forward to going home. Since he had taken on Joshua Banks as a client, there had been a tension between him and

Angela. He clearly felt that she thought he was working for the wrong side. When Brent pulled into the driveway at home, he was happy to find Angela's car outside. *Not another night with just me and the cat.*

He exited the car with excitement, but still held some trepidation because of the tensions they had had lately. Those apprehensions were allayed almost the minute he walked in the door, as Angela came to him immediately and gave him a huge, warm hug.

"That's a great homecoming."

They broke the embrace, and Angela kissed him.

"How did it go today?"

"Rough."

"Why don't you go get cleaned up and then tell me all about it? Or just go get cleaned up and ..."

"I think I like the second one better."

\*\*\*

Jack sent a quick voice text to Brent. "I'm tailing Clairborne. He's on the move. Give you more when I get it." Jack disconnected, threw the phone on the passenger seat, and turned his attention back to Clairborne, who pulled off the freeway on Kuehner Drive and turned right.

*He's probably headed for Sage Park.*

Finally, when Clairborne pulled onto Black Canyon Road, Jack's suspicions were confirmed. Sage Ranch Park was a rugged 625-acre park in the northwestern Simi Hills. It was popular among hikers, infested with snakes, and a great jump-off spot for someone who wanted to step off the grid for a while without going too far from home.

The park was nearly deserted, as usual. Clairborne took his car as far as it would go. Jack found a spot about half a mile away to hide and observe him. Clairborne didn't waste any time. He got out his backpack and rifled through the boxes to pack it completely full.

*Going hiking?* Jack zoomed in on Clairborne with his telephoto lens and took pictures.

Finally, Dusty locked up his car and hit the dusty trail. Jack slipped out of his car and followed carefully behind Clairborne as he hiked through the mountain park. After about an hour of hiking and tracking, just as it was getting dark, Clairborne found a place to camp and pitched his tent. Jack knew that this stakeout had just taken on a new dimension, and that it would not include a marshmallow roast.

# CHAPTER THIRTY NINE

The evening with Angela was just what Brent needed, but the morning left him in doubt about what he was doing. True, every criminal defendant needed a defense, but this was not Brent's "thing" anymore. He had struggled through small-time criminal cases in his "dues paying" days. *Do I really want to make my mark on society like this? Here lies Brent Marks, shyster to the bad guys.* Brent knew he didn't want this to be his legacy, but there was something that had always bothered him about the Banks case. Sure, Banks was a nut - a whole can of nuts; but the chips in the case just weren't adding up. So, Brent resolved to set aside his own doubts about the innocence of his client and finish the job he had started.

Back in court, Bradley Chernow barreled on with the prosecution. He had taken the entire first week, and his case was going well into Tuesday at full steam. Chernow called the blood spatter expert, who reconstructed the anatomy of the murder for the jury. Brent had only a few questions on cross-examination, as the physicality of the murder itself was not the focal point of his defense. Doctor Perez was called, and discussed his autopsy report and the cause of the deaths of James and Ronald Bennett. More gory facts for the jury to digest. Brent emphasized on cross the fact that the fatal damage was caused by a large, military-style knife that had never been found. But this was a case of emotional impact over evidence - which was sorely lacking in the prosecution.

Chernow called all the members of the forensic team in the case. The clothes Banks were wearing were confirmed to have the blood of both victims on them. Joshua Banks himself exhibited no likable personality characteristics for the jury. *If I don't like him, how is the jury ever going to care about what happens to him?* He sat at counsel table and whispered a question to Brent every once and a while. Susan Fredericks sat in the second row of the gallery every day with her constant glare of contempt, which was clearly visible to the jury, directed at Banks.

Chernow called Angela to the stand to reinforce the findings of the task force against Joshua Banks. It was difficult for Brent to cross-examine her, but her testimony was fairly dry and cumulative; so his questions were short and to the point. He also called Detective Rhonda Salas to the stand to testify, despite the fact that he knew Brent would try to turn her into his own witness on cross-examination. Brent jumped on the opportunity.

"Detective Salas, you attended training at the Allan Hancock Police & Fire Academy and the program at the Ventura County Justice Center and graduated top of your class, didn't you?"

"Yes, I did."

"And you've also had specialized training in self-defense and hand-to-hand combat?"

"Yes, I have had martial arts training."

"Did part of your training include how to disarm a suspect in a knife attack?"

"Yes."

"Detective Salas, you were the victim of an attack by the alleged Honeymoon Killer, were you not?"

"Yes, I was."

Salas played it plain and dry. It was up to Brent to try to elicit some emotion from her.

"According to your report, the attack occurred in your bed, while you were sleeping?"

"That's right."

Then Brent broke the cardinal rule of cross-examination: never ask a question that doesn't call for a "yes" or "no" answer.

"Detective Salas, please tell the jury what happened during that attack."

Salas looked surprised.

"From the beginning?"

"Yes."

"The suspect attacked me in my bed."

*Not dry and boring, Salas! Make us feel it!*

"He came at you with a knife?"

"Yes."

"Did you seem him coming?"

"Yes, I was sleeping lightly, I heard something and I saw shadows in the hallway."

"And you prepared yourself for an attack?"

"Yes."

"How?" Brent elevated his voice.

"I pressed the panic button on my police radio. But I couldn't get to my gun."

"Why not?"

"It was locked in the gun safe."

"And a gun is not a very good defender against a knife attack, is it?"

"No."

"Why not?"

"Because, by the time you get a bearing and take aim, the attacker has already had a chance to cut you."

"And he cut you, didn't he?"

"Yes, he did." Salas's voice started to waiver. She was back in the memory.

"Where did he cut you?"

"My shoulder."

"You must have been afraid."

"I was terrified."

*Now we're getting somewhere.*

"In fact, Detective Salas, if you had not defended the first attack, he would have killed you, isn't that correct?"

"Objection, calls for speculation."

"Overruled, you may answer."

"Yes, he would have killed me."

"How did you protect yourself from his attack?"

"I kicked him as hard as I could."

"Where?"

"Right in his balls, that's where!"

*That's it, Rhonda. Bring it home.*

"Then what happened?"

"Then I rolled out of the way and got on my feet, but that maniac kept coming at me. I grabbed a pillow to try to deflect the knife, and he sliced right through it and kept coming. I knew I was going to get cut again and that he was going to kill me unless I did something, so I arched back so he couldn't reach me with the knife, but I could still do something with my hands. I could feel the air from the knife as he swept it within inches of my abdomen. Then I grabbed his wrist with my right hand and immobilized it for a split second while I hit his hand as hard as I could with my left, and the he dropped the knife."

"Was he powerful?"

"He was extremely powerful. I could hardly hold the grip on his wrist. I was just lucky I was able to do it so quickly. I learned how to do it in my martial arts training."

"Then, what did you do?"

"I ran for my life."

"Did you get a good look at the suspect?"

"Yes, but he was dressed in black and he wore a mask."

"Was he a big man?"

"I thought he was. He seemed about six-five or six-six - but I was in shock, so I'm not sure how accurate that is."

"He towered over you?"

"Yes."

"And you're about what, five-eight?"

"Exactly."

"And were you able to approximate his weight?"

"At the time, it seemed he was about 230 to 235 pounds; but, still, I can't be sure."

"Detective Salas, would you please step down from the witness box?"

"Objection, Your Honor."

"Counsel approach."

At the bench, Brent argued in favor of his demonstration, and the judge allowed it.

"Detective Salas, please stand in front of the witness stand."   Salas took her place as instructed.

"May I approach, Your Honor?"

"Proceed, Mr. Marks."

"Mr. Banks, please come and join us."  Banks did as he was instructed.

"Stand here."   Brent motioned to a spot opposite Salas.  Brent looked at the jury to make sure they were paying attention.  Salas and Banks stood almost head to head.

"Detective, this was not the person who attacked you, was it?"

"Objection!  Argumentative!"

"Sustained. The jury will disregard the question. Do you have any further questions for this witness, Mr. Marks?"

"Not at this time, Your Honor."

"Mr. Chernow?"

"Thank you, Your Honor. Detective, you were traumatized by this attack, weren't you?"

"Severely."

"Were you in psychological counseling after the attack?"

"Yes, I was."

"For how long?"

"About six weeks."

"How long did the attack last, from when he first jumped at you in your bed until you ran out the door?"

"I would say less than 30 seconds."

"And you were asleep when he first attacked, is that correct?"

"Yes."

"So, you had less than 30 seconds to kick your attacker in the groin, disarm him, and run away. How many seconds of that was spent observing him?"

"I would say only a few seconds."

"Less than three seconds?"

"Probably."

"So, you had less than three seconds to assess the height and weight of your attacker?"

"Objection! Leading: asked and answered and bordering on argumentative."

"Sustained. The jury will disregard the question."

"Detective, would you say that you had an adequate opportunity to estimate the height and weight of your attacker?"

"Certainly less than I usually have."

"Thank you. No further questions, Your Honor."

"Mr. Marks, re-cross?"

"Thank you, Your Honor."

Brent stood up and approached the well.

"Detective Salas, part of your training you received in the two police academies you attended involved developing your powers of observation, is that correct?"

"Yes."

"And you have been on the job for over ten years, isn't that correct?"

"Yes, I have."

"And during those ten years you have written hundreds of arrest reports, isn't that correct?"

"Yes, I have."

"Over 500?"

"At least."

"Your powers of observation enable you to determine the physical characteristics of a suspect in several seconds, do they not?"

"Not necessarily. It depends."

"Were you trained in the correct use of your firearm?"

"Yes."

"Did that include obstacle course training?"

"Yes, it did."

"Do you take periodic refresher firearms training?"

"Yes."

"How often?"

"Four times a year."

"And does that include obstacle course firearms training?"

"Yes."

"Detective, in the obstacle course, are you presented with mannequin targets which pop out, representing criminals with firearms?"

"Yes."

"And are these randomly interspersed with other mannequins who pop out at you during the course, which represent ordinary unarmed citizens?"

"Yes."

"Are you required to ascertain the difference in a matter of less than one second to determine if you should shoot at the target or not?"

"Yes."

"May I approach, Your Honor?"

"Yes."

Brent approached the witness stand and placed an exhibit before Detective Salas.

"Showing you a document marked for identification as Defense Exhibit C, can you identify this?"

"It's the records of my obstacle course performance."

"And these records show a 90% accuracy score over the past three years?"

"They do."

"Detective Salas, you were asked on redirect whether you sought psychological therapy after your attack, correct?"

"Yes."

"Isn't it true that this therapy was required as a condition of your coming back to duty after the attack?"

"Yes."

"Nothing further, Your Honor."

# CHAPTER FORTY

Jack watched as the light from the lantern inside the tent waned and finally died off. It was difficult to be patient: his lips were parched and his stomach was growling. He had finished the last bit of water he had brought from his car and was getting thirsty. His phone had a good three bars on it and a full battery, so he sent a text to Brent to keep him up to date. *Stalking Clairborne in Sage Park. No details to report yet.*

Jack gave it a good two hours before making his move. Using just the light of the half moon, he crept toward the tent and listened for any sounds inside. With one hand on his gun, he used his free hand to peel open the flap of the tent.

# CHAPTER FORTY ONE

Brent awoke at about 5 a.m. and checked his phone. Nothing from Jack. He texted him. *Jack, what's going on? Are you still in the wilderness?* Then, he closed his eyes and pondered whether to get up or try to get some more sleep. After thirty minutes of tossing and turning, it seemed that sleep was not going to return, so he got up. He checked the phone again. Still nothing from Jack. Brent had to prepare for court, so he sent Jack a quick message: *Jack, please check in; worried about you. Getting ready for court now.*

By the time court had reconvened, Brent received a text back from Jack: *Still working on it.* Brent responded back with: *Starting our defense today. Critical that we get something.*

Brent started his case-in-chief by calling Dr. Jean Beverly, who had put together a psychological profile of the murderer and discussed how Banks differed from that profile.

"Dr. Beverly, did you examine Joshua Banks?"

"Yes, on two separate occasions."

"In your opinion, what were the similarities and differences between your profile of the killer and Mr. Banks?"

"Only differences. Banks' history did not reveal any physical injuries or physical or mental abuse. He reported a normal childhood, with the exception that his family was extremely religious. He had no history of acting out violent fantasies on animals; in fact, he was quite repulsed by the suggestion of it. He also had no history of voyeurism or fetishism and his sexual history was almost devoid of masturbation. He has no history of alcohol or drug abuse. Many of these traits are historically found in serial killers.

"Mr. Banks exhibited no traits of compulsive control or manipulation. While he has an obsession with religion, he doesn't appear to have any psychopathological or antisocial personality disorder. In the context of his church meetings and events, he is actually very social. He is humble, rather than egotistical. In short, he exhibits none of the traits of a serial killer, in my opinion."

Brent had to reveal that Banks was just a different colored nut in the can; but that didn't make him a murderer.

"Dr. Beverly, Mr. Banks is different than most of us, isn't he, though?"

"Certainly, he is very eccentric, especially with regard to his religious beliefs; but, although this has distanced him from many people, he doesn't exhibit the sociopathic or psychopathic behavior you would expect to see from a serial killer. I diagnosed him with obsessive compulsive disorder and referred him to a colleague of mine, Father Brown, who has experience in counseling people with religious obsessions."

On cross-examination, Chernow chewed up Dr. Beverly's testimony.

"Dr. Beverly, you've testified that the defendant doesn't fit the serial killer profile, but that doesn't mean that he could not have committed these murders, does it?"

"Well, it would be inconsistent with the profile."

"But you can't say, with a degree of certainty, that there is no way that the defendant could have committed these murders, can you?"

"No, I can't."

"Thank you." Chernow smiled at the jury confidently and took his seat.

By the lunch break, Brent had still not heard from Jack, and all of his texts since the morning had gone unanswered.

\*\*\*

Brent ended the day with Dr. Jaime Orozco. Dr. Orozco had over 30 years' experience as a pathologist and medical examiner. He had degrees in medicine and law and experience as the Chief Medical Examiner for the County of Los Angeles, and 10 years with the FBI. He was highly qualified to give a medical opinion.

Orozco testified that he had tested Banks' blood on the day he had turned himself in, and the test results had revealed abnormally high levels of PCP. However, none of the drug was found on his person.

"PCP, or phencyclidine, is called 'angel dust' on the street. It is an extremely strong hallucinogen that can be smoked, insufflated, injected, or taken orally."

"Did you conduct a brief physical examination of Mr. Banks?"

"Yes, I did."

"And, as a result of your examination, were you able to form an opinion, to a reasonable degree of medical certainty, on how Mr. Banks had ingested the PCP?"

"Yes, I did."

"Please tell the jury your opinion and its basis."

Dr. Orozco spoke to the jury as though he were speaking to a group of friends at his dinner table.

"I found no track marks in the skin which would have revealed that the drug was injected. If smoked, PCP is usually used as a dip for a marijuana or tobacco cigarette, and there was no evidence of such in his blood work. There was no powder present in his nasal passages, so it was not likely that he insufflated it. It is my opinion that it was orally ingested."

"Is PCP often used as a date rape drug?"

"Objection, lack of foundation."

"Overruled. Doctor, you may answer, if you have an opinion."

"Yes: because its effects can include anesthesia, it is often used as such. It is usually dissolved in a drink or food."

"Once administered, does it make the subject easier to manipulate?"

"Oh, yes. Due to its anesthetic effect, the subject would have little or no control over his or her own body."

Chernow, on cross examination, took advantage of the other effects of PCP.

"Doctor, isn't it true that other effects of PCP besides the anesthetic effect include aggressive behavior?"

"Occasionally, yes."

"And do they also include paranoia and depersonalization?"

"Yes."

"What is depersonalization, doctor?"

"It is the state of being detached from oneself, as if the world has become less real or lacking in significance."

*He's turning the doctor against us!*

"So if somebody in this state of mind did something, he or she may not be sure if it was really happening or if was just a fantasy or a dream?"

"It is possible, yes."

"Thank you, doctor. No further questions, Your Honor."

"Mr. Marks?"

"Thank you, Your Honor. Doctor, in the state in which you observed Mr. Banks on the night of your examination, in your opinion, was he capable of taking care of himself?"

"No: he was hallucinating and lacked general physical coordination."

"Was he, in your opinion, physically capable of overpowering someone else?"

"No, he was barely able to stand up."

"Thank you."

Still no word from Jack. After court, Brent whipped out his cell phone and called Jack. No answer. His previous texts, however, were showing that they had been received. *What's going on, Jack?* Five minutes later, he received a reply: *Still working on it, looks like a dead end.* Brent texted back: *Keep trying, we're dead without it. See you in court tomorrow.*

# CHAPTER FORTY TWO

Brent called Detective David Maloney as his next witness, and Chernow blew a gasket.

"Your Honor, I object to this witness on the grounds of relevance. Plus, he's not on the initial witness list."

"Your Honor, may we approach?"

Brent explained to the judge that he had just found out about Maloney during Chernow's case-in-chief and summarized his agreement with Chernow for discovery on the stolen vehicle lead, and that Brent would be able to call investigators as witnesses as part of his case.

"But this is a different case, Your Honor. Counsel is not playing fair here."

"On the contrary, Mr. Chernow, it seems to fall within the purview of your agreement. I'm going to allow this witness."

Brent and Chernow resumed their battle positions. Brent checked his text messages for anything from Jack. There was one that had come in about 8 a.m. that said, "Still working, will keep you posted." *Damn it, Jack!* Brent had to turn his attention back to the case. As Charles Stinson always said: "No distractions, boy. When you're in a trial, you eat, drink, sleep and shit only the case."

Detective Maloney was a young man in his 30s, dressed in the usual detective garb of white shirt, black tie, and grey slacks; and he had added a touch of his own: a grey sports jacket.

"Detective Maloney, you are a California peace officer employed by the Santa Barbara County Sheriff's Department: is that correct?"

"Yes."

"And how long have you been a detective?"

"I've passed the exam about a year now."

"Congratulations, Detective."

"Thanks." Maloney beamed, and his cheeks turned red.

"Detective, to what detail are you assigned in the Sheriff's Department?"

"The stolen property detail."

"So when someone suffers a theft, they come to you for the police report to give to their insurance company: is that right?"

"That's one of our functions. We also investigate auto theft."

"I see. Now, that's where you come in to this case. Did you investigate the theft of a large, heavy-duty tow truck that was reported stolen from J.C. Riley and Sons Towing in May of this year?"

"Yes, I did."

"How did you get assigned to this case?"

"It was a cold lead, out of homicide."

"By cold lead, do you mean it's something the homicide division was working on that was referred to you because they determined it wasn't involved with one of their cases?"

"Yes."

"Who assigned you this cold lead?"

"Detective Tomassi."

Brent had Maloney identify the police reports on the stolen tow truck, and admitted them into evidence.

"It says in these reports, Detective, that there was a suspect in this case."

"Objection, Your Honor. Irrelevant."

"Overruled. You may answer, Detective."

"Yes: Dusty Clairborne, an employee of the tow yard."

"Did you interview Mr. Clairborne?"

"No."

"Was he ever arrested?"

"No."

"I'm showing you now defense exhibit G, which are Dusty Clairborne's personnel records subpoenaed from the custodian of records of J.C. Riley and Sons. Calling your attention to page 2, paragraph 3: does the description of six foot six inches and 230 pounds match the description of the suspect in your police reports?"

Maloney flipped through the reports.

"Yes, it does."

"Now, Detective, I'm going to play the surveillance video from the discovery package I received from Mr. Chernow. Please call your attention to the overhead screen."

Brent played the surveillance video.

"Detective Maloney, did you do any investigation to determine the identity of the person in this video?"

"No, I didn't."

"Why not?"

"Because when we blew up the video, there was no visible face. We had nothing to go on but the video. It could have been anybody. There were no latent prints inside the truck when we recovered it."

"So you closed the case?"

"Yes, we closed it as unsolved."

Chernow couldn't do much on cross-examination, so his questions were limited.

"Mr. Marks, please call your next witness."

"Thank you, Your Honor. I call Dr. Michael Kensington."

Dr. Kensington took his seat in the witness stand and made eye contact with the jury while listening to Brent's questioning.

"Dr. Kensington, can you please summarize your background and experience?"

"Certainly. I hold a Bachelor of Science from Columbia University, a Masters in Science from Stanford and a PhD. in Computer Science from Yale University. I have published several papers on digital video analysis, optical flow estimation, and human shape and motion analysis."

Dr. Kensington testified as an expert of human shape reconstruction from two-dimensional images. He disclosed that he had been hired by the defense team at a rate of $450 per hour for his reports and $650 per hour for his testimony.

"Your Honor, I object to this witness on the grounds of unfair surprise."

"Counsel, please approach."

Brent and Chernow went to the bench for a conference outside the hearing range of the jury.

"Mr. Marks, do you have an offer of proof?"

"Yes, Your Honor, I do. Mr. Chernow provided me with an updated discovery package which included the surveillance video of the tow yard last week, during his case-in-chief. We've talked about this before, Your Honor. In order to actually do something with this evidence, I had to hire an expert to estimate the height and weight of the figure in the video who is thought to be the person who stole the tow truck. It was extremely difficult to find an expert who could do the analysis and be available to testify on such short notice."

"Your Honor, I have not been provided with a copy of this expert's report or qualifications in a timely manner."

"Your Honor, with all due respect, that is not true. As soon as we were able to identify the expert, we updated our witness list and provided Mr. Chernow with a copy of the witness's C.V. We didn't have the report until this morning, and I gave a copy of it to Mr. Chernow as soon as I received it myself."

"Mr. Chernow, I'm going to allow the expert to testify. If the prosecution had been more forthcoming with the discovery, it would not be in the pickle that it's in now. However, I will give you time, if you wish, to review the report and attempt to obtain your own expert. You can call your expert as part of your rebuttal."

Chernow pouted like a small child who had been refused an ice cream cone, but he had to respond with 'Thank You, Your Honor.'

"Thank You, Your Honor."

"We will take our afternoon break now, a little early, so that you can coordinate with your office."

# CHAPTER FORTY THREE

*Where the hell are you, Jack?* Brent furiously texted on his iPhone. Then he called Angela.

"Hey, Angie."

"Hi, Brent. How's the trial going?"

"It's going. I've just lost track of Jack."

"Is he still in the field?"

"Yeah, but he knows I need him in court today."

"I'm sure he'll be there. Has he checked in at all?"

"He's been texting."

"I'm sure he has a good reason for not being there yet."

"I hope so."

"You want to meet for lunch? I can be there in five minutes."

"No, thanks. I'm going to work through lunch."

Brent called Jack at least six times during the break. His last message registered as "received," but Jack had still not texted back. Finally, just as he was headed back to court, Brent received a response: *Still working a lead. Your going to be happy.*

*Strange. Jack knows how to spell 'you're'. Must be his spell checker gone cuckoo. No time to think about it now. Have to get back inside.*

Dr. Kensington resumed his place in the witness chair, and Brent approached him.

"Dr. Kensington, were you able estimate the size and weight of the man in the surveillance video, Defense Exhibit H?"

"Yes, I was."

"Can you tell the jury how you determined this estimate?"

Kensington turned his view to the jury and explained carefully.

"In this case, we were lucky to have a known background in the video. I was able to visit the tow yard, calculate the distance of the video camera from the background, and take measurements of the background for scale purposes. This allowed me to make an extraction of an accurate foreground silhouette of the figure in the video."

"Can you show the jury how you did this, Doctor?"

"Of course. Can you please project the image of my laptop screen?"

The Bailiff flipped a switch and the screen next to the witness box was illuminated.

"As you can see here, the measurements of the background were input into this three-dimensional model, which I constructed from the video imagery. That, including the distance that I calculated from the camera to the background, gave me an accurate scale of size.

"I then estimated the shape and size of the body represented by the image, using information from the image such as joint position and size to scale, which allowed me to create this three-dimensional figure of the subject in this model."

"Were you able to form an opinion of the sex, height and weight of the individual depicted in the video, within a reasonable degree of scientific certainty?"

"Yes. I was able to do so with an accuracy factor of 97%."

"What is your opinion, Doctor?"

"It is my opinion that the subject depicted by the image in the video is a male, with an approximate height of six feet six inches, and an approximate weight of 235 pounds."

"So, your opinion essentially matches the description of Detective Salas of her attacker."

"Objection, argumentative."

"Sustained. Mr. Marks, it's about five minutes to five. How much longer do you figure you have on direct?"

"I'm actually done, Your Honor."

"In that case, court will recess now, for the day, and Mr. Chernow can cross examine Dr. Kensington first thing tomorrow morning."

# CHAPTER FORTY FOUR

Brent headed straight for Jack's place after court. Jack's car was not there. He found his spare key under a flower pot on the back porch and let himself in. He looked around. There was no sign that Jack had been there that day or the night before. It looked like he had left his home on vacation or something. He logged on to Jack's laptop computer, and activated the "find your iPhone" feature. Jack's iPhone was still at Sage Ranch Park. *He must still be following Clairborne.*

Jack was on the move. Since Brent couldn't reach him, he decided to just go to him. He noted the GPS coordinates of the iPhone, programmed them into his own iPhone and set off to find Jack. Brent stopped by his house and took the precaution of dressing in his hiking gear and stocked a backpack with some water and snacks and the Beretta that he had bought for protection when Joshua Banks had threatened him years ago.

Brent crept up Black Canyon Road until he found Jack's car, but the GPS coordinates for it were different than the ones from his iPhone. *He must be on foot.* He felt the hood of the car. It was cold. *Not been moved for a while.* Jack's was not the only car there. There was also an old AMC Pacer. *Jack said Clairborne was driving a Pacer.* Brent had always hated the way they looked. Thankfully, there were so few of them on the road now, he figured that this one had to belong to Clairborne. He parked his car away from the others, got out of it, and got his backpack out of the trunk. As Brent started to follow the GPS coordinates down the hiking trail, he had a thought. *Flat tires are always a pain in the butt. Always slowing you down.* Brent realized for a moment that he should have some kind of backup, so he phoned Angela.

"You're doing *what*?"

"Well, Angie, everyone - including you - thinks that this is a wild goose chase, but I have a feeling that Jack may be in trouble. That's why I'm calling."

"Stay there. I'll call Tomassi and we'll arrange a search party."

"I think I'd better just call 9-1-1 once I've located Jack. I just wanted to keep you posted."

"Brent, be careful. Don't do anything foolish."

*I can't promise that.*

"Bye, Angie."

Brent disconnected and, using his pocketknife, let the air out of Clairborne's right front tire until it was nice and flat. Then he followed the coordinates down the hiking trail. Suddenly, right in front of him, was a large rattlesnake, slinking through the sandy trail. Brent stopped quickly, so as not to step on it, and carefully walked around it.

Finally, after about an hour of hiking, the coordinates led him off the hiking trail. Brent followed them, carefully blazing his own trail in the brush and looking for snakes as he went along. The GPS coordinates pointed him to a deep ravine. There was no sign of Jack anywhere. Brent crawled down to the bottom. Again, no sign of Jack. *Wait! There's a phone!* Brent reached down to pick up a dusty and damaged iPhone. *It's Jack's!*

The sun would be setting in the next two hours, and after that, it would be impossible to find Jack. Brent figured his best bet would be to get back on the makeshift trail and wait there. *Clairborne is still out there. I wonder if he has Jack.*

Brent climbed back up to the trail. He waited for a while, but couldn't stand the thought of doing nothing while Jack was out there somewhere. *But, there's no way I can cover this whole wilderness park.*

Brent decided that the most logical thing to do would be to go back to the cars. He retraced his steps until he got back to the main trail, and followed it back. Clairborne's car was still there.

Brent called 9-1-1.

"My friend has been lost hiking in Sage Park. I think he may be in danger."

"We'll send the Fire Department."

"You'd better send the police as well. He's an armed retired FBI agent and he's been following an armed and dangerous subject."

"Stay where you are. Help is on the way."

Brent put his backpack into the trunk and sat in his car, waiting, sipping on water and holding his gun in his hand. *I'd better put it away before they get here.*

Just holding the gun felt scary. Brent had taken lessons on firing it and was a fairly accurate shot. But that was shooting at targets. Shooting at another human being was an entirely different thing.

Just then, a tall figure appeared at the opening of the trail. *It's Clairborne!*

Brent grabbed his gun, tucked it in his belt, popped his trunk, got out of the car, and put his backpack on. As Clairborne approached his car, Brent smiled and waved.

"Hey, buddy. Do you know any good trails out here?"

Clairborne glared at him. "I'm not your buddy. It's too late to be hiking anyway. Just leave me alone." Clairborne noticed the flat tire and grumbled. He took off his pack and put it on the ground next to the car, then went to his trunk and got out the spare tire and jack gear.

"Need some help with that?"

"Didn't I tell you to leave me alone?" Clairborne crouched on the ground and started to position the jack under the wheel. Brent cocked the Beretta and pointed it at his head.

"I'm afraid I can't do that, Dusty."

Clairborne turned, brandishing a tire iron.

"Drop it!"

Brent could hear the sounds of sirens in the distance. He didn't know if they were police, or firemen, or both.

"And if I don't?"

"First, hear the sirens? I called 9-1-1 and those are the cops coming. Second, unless you can throw that tire iron faster than I can shoot you in the head, I would drop it if you want to live."

"So, if I don't, you'll shoot me?"

"Try me!" Brent fired a shot into the rear tire, and it exploded. Clairborne dropped the tire iron.

"Now put your hands on your head, and kick that backpack over to me."

Clairborne kicked the backpack over. Brent kept the gun trained on him as he spilled the contents onto the ground. Among the things that came clattering out was a large K-Bar knife and a 9mm handgun.

"Nice knife. And that looks like Jack Ruder's gun. Where is he?"

"That's an illegal search."

"Really, Mr. Know-it-all? I'm not a cop. And when the cops do come, which I'd say will be in about two minutes, they're going to see all this stuff in plain sight. No search at all. Now where's Jack?"

Clairborne grinned. Brent saw his crazy cold eyes. He picked up the knife, screamed, "God will protect me!" and ran at Brent, waving the knife in front of him. Brent fired, but the big man kept coming. He fired again, and again, in rapid succession, missing once, then hitting Clairborne in the chest, neck and head. Blood spewed everywhere, and Clairborne fell only a few feet away from Brent, whose entire body was shaking.

"Police! Drop your weapon!"

"Brent looked up to see two police officers, with guns drawn, and dropped his gun. He froze.

"Hands on your head!"

Brent put his hands on his head.

"On your knees." Brent dropped to his knees. He knew at that moment they were going to take him down. With the force of an NFL linebacker, one of the officers slammed into Brent, pushing his face into the dust and grabbing his arms. The officer handcuffed Brent and stood him up.

313

"I'm the one who called you."

The search and rescue team found Jack before darkness had set in. His ankle had been broken and he was dehydrated. His electrolytes were extremely low and he wouldn't have made it through the next day. Clairborne had been messaging Brent so as not to arouse any suspicion, then had thrown Jack's iPhone away. Brent was held for questioning, then released.

The current events had changed the entire strategy of the trial. Bradley Chernow surely had to agree to dismiss the case. Brent couldn't make a motion for directed verdict (a procedure used in civil cases which took the case away from the jury for lack of sufficient evidence) because, unlike other states, California law did not allow it in criminal cases. Brent simply had to have faith that Chernow, given the new evidence, would do the right thing.

# CHAPTER FORTY FIVE

Brent barely made it to court on time. He looked as if he had slept in his suit, even though he had not slept at all. When Chernow entered the courtroom, he gave Brent a strange look.

"You look like crap, Marks."

"Thanks, Brad. I'm not sure if you know it yet, but I solved your case last night."

Brent filled Brad in with all the details of the past 12 hours.

"That's an incredible story, Marks. But it still won't get you out of this trial. Your guy's guilty and he's going down."

"You've got to be kidding!"

"On the contrary. As far as circumstantial evidence goes, I think we have a winner. And you've got nothing. Let's see what the jury says."

Before the judge took the bench and before the jury was brought in, Brent requested a conference with the judge. Sitting in her chambers, Brent laid out his offer of proof.

"Mr. Chernow, are you sure there's no way to settle this case?"

"He wants a dismissal, Your Honor."

"I don't like the way this looks, Mr. Chernow. I'm powerless at this point, and can't take this case away from the jury, but I strongly suggest that the two of you talk it over and try to resolve it."

"I'll do life with possibility of parole, Your Honor. That's as far as we can go."

"You really think your case is that strong, given this new evidence?"

"I'm not sure what this *new evidence* shows, Your Honor. I'm sure the police will get to the bottom of this Clairborne fellow and whatever crimes he committed, along with investigating Mr. Marks for shooting him."

"Thanks, Brad."

316

"Really, Marks, you think you can blow someone away and just walk?"

"Gentlemen, this isn't helping us in this case. Please take the next half hour to discuss it, and if you can't settle it, be prepared to go on with your case, Mr. Marks."

***

"I call Jack Ruder, Your Honor."

Jack was wheeled in front of the jury in a wheelchair, still bearing the scars from his ordeal. He testified how his investigation of Dusty Clairborne had led him to follow Clairborne to Sage Ranch Park.

Brent went over Jack's background as an ex-LAPD cop and ex-FBI agent who had served on several serial killer task forces. Jack walked the jury through his investigation, starting at the point where Dusty Clairborne had become a suspect.

"Please tell the jury what happened while you were conducting surveillance on Dusty Clairborne?"

"Unfortunately, Mr. Clairborne discovered I was following him, and he set a trap for me."

Brent paused for a moment to let the jury anticipate Jack's story. All of their curious eyes were on Jack.

"What kind of a trap?"

*Clairborne was sure someone was following him. It couldn't just be another hiker. This one was going out of his way to make sure he wasn't seen. He ran ahead, climbed a large eucalyptus tree, and waited.*

*Jack rounded the curve. He'd lost track of Clairborne. He looked to the left and right sides of the trail. No luck. Jack determined to trudge on.*

*Clairborne saw Jack approaching, and hid in the camouflage of the tree, waiting for the perfect moment. Jack continued on the trail, until he was right under the eucalyptus tree.*

*As Jack passed under the tree, Clairborne pounced on him.*

*The wind was knocked out of Jack. He felt the weight of the man on top of him and could smell his foul body order and bad breath.*

*"Why are you following me?"*

*"What are you talking about?"*

*Jack's arms were pinned down with the big man's knees. Clairborne rifled through his pockets, finding his wallet and iPhone.*

*"I'm talkin about this, Mr. FBI man." Clairborne held Jack's retired FBI ID in front of his face. He then searched Jack for a gun, and of course, found it in his shoulder holster.*

*Clairborne got off of Jack, and pointed Jack's gun at him.*

*"Get up, FBI Man!"*

*Jack struggled to stand up, but couldn't put his weight on his left ankle.*

*"I can't. I think my ankle's broken."*

*Clairborne pulled Jack by the arm to his feet.*

*"Looks like it works just fine. Move!"*

*Clairborne pointed the gun at Jack, who limped along, dragging his injured leg.*

*"Keep moving!"*

*"What's your plan?"*

*"I'm walkin' out of here alone, that's my plan."*

*"I called for backup, you know. They're on the way."*

*Clairborne laughed. "Your backup sounds like it's going to be a while in coming.*

"Clairborne had my iPhone and was replying to your texts, so you would think that I was okay."

"What did he do next?"

"After forcing me to drag my broken ankle for about an hour on that hiking trail, he wiped my phone off and threw it into a ravine. Then he made me continue."

*Jack couldn't walk anymore. He fell to the ground.*

*"Not here! Get up!"*

*Clairborne kicked Jack in the ribs, and he groaned and fell in a cloud of dust. Clairborne kept kicking, shoving him with his foot until Jack tumbled down off the trail, into another ravine.*

"And he left me there to die."

# CHAPTER FORTY SIX

"That story is all very interesting, Mr. Ruder. But it still doesn't explain what connection, if any, that Dusty Clairborne has to this case."

"Objection, argumentative!"

"Sustained. The jury will disregard the question. Please keep your questions without argument, Mr. Chernow."

"Thank you, Your Honor. Mr. Ruder, isn't it correct that your investigation of Mr. Clairborne did not uncover any evidence that directly connects him with this case?"

"No, that is not correct..."

Chernow looked surprised. Because he had his own blinders on, he had broken the cardinal rule of cross-examination as well as trial preparation. He had asked a question without knowing what the answer would be.

"...The police discovered, among his possessions, a military-style K-Bar knife. It's being tested in the crime lab now."

"Objection and move to strike, Your Honor. These facts are not in evidence."

"I am calling one of the officers who responded to the scene, Your Honor. He's my next witness."

"I'm going to sustain the objection for now, Mr. Marks, subject to you connecting it up with the next witness. The jury is instructed to disregard Mr. Ruder's answer."

That error threw Chernow off for the rest of the cross-examination. For the rest of the story, since Brent could not testify himself, he called Officer Kevin Huckavy, a young Simi Valley patrolman with a military style haircut. Huckavy had been on the job for a little over three years. He had seen enough to not be surprised by anything yet, but still had the vigor, promise, and optimism of a new recruit. He was as excited to tell the story as Jack was. Huckavy told the jury how he had responded to the scene of the 9-1-1 call that had been placed by Brent.

"When we came on the scene, Mr. Marks had just shot Dusty Clairborne. We secured Marks in restraints and ascertained that Clairborne was dead."

All members of the jury were now looking at Brent with great surprise. They had not expected the saga to take this turn.

"Did you take an inventory of Mr. Clairborne's personal property?"

"Yes, we did."

"And is this inventory in your report?"

"Yes, it is."

"Officer, I am showing you a copy of what has been marked for identification as Defense Exhibit W. Can you identify this document?"

"Yes, that is my report on the Dusty Clairborne incident."

"Included in the inventory was a knife, is that correct?"

"Yes."

"Can you describe the knife?"

"It is a military-issue KA-BAR knife with a seven inch blade."

Brent projected a photograph of the knife onto the overhead screen.

"Did you take this photograph of the knife for your report?"

"I did."

"Your Honor, the defense moves Exhibit W into evidence."

"No objection? It is received."

"Thank you, Your Honor. I have no further questions for this witness."

"Mr. Chernow?"

"Officer Huckavy, isn't it true that no blood was found on the knife?"

"Yes. It is in the lab for analysis now."

"But the blade and handle appeared to be clear of any blood, isn't that correct?"

"Yes, that is correct."

Brent had delivered a sufficient dose of reasonable doubt. The question was, at this point, whether to risk calling Banks as a witness. Wrapped up in his convoluted mind was an explanation of how he had been found in the blood-stained clothes. Loose ends were the worst part of any trial presentation. There was no other way to get that explanation to the jury.

Brent met with Banks in the holding cell after court to discuss his possible testimony. The crazy man was wide-eyed and excited.

"Mr. Banks, I know I said I didn't want you to testify, but it may be the only way to explain how you got into those blood-stained clothes."

"God provided me the clothes. And the way out!" Banks was animated. He truly believed this.

"And how did you get out of the bus?"

"The demon! He descended upon me with his foul breath. I awoke and he was standing over me!"

Brent showed Banks a picture of Dusty Clairborne. "Do you recognize this, Mr. Banks?"

Banks turned his head away in fear.

"That is the demon! In his human form, without the horns."

"And you've seen him with the horns?"

"Of course. I was a prisoner of the demon for many days."

"Mr. Banks, if you testify, we have to work on your presentation."

"My presentation?"

"Yes, some details.  Well, we just have to leave them out.  Make it simple.  Do you think you can do that?"

"If it is God's will, I can do it."

"Then we should pray that it is God's will."

# CHAPTER FORTY SEVEN

Brent met with Banks for two hours that evening at the jail. After the meeting, he was hungry and exhausted. Thankfully, Angela was waiting for him at home. Brent walked in the door. He was pale as if all the blood had been drained from his face. He felt faint, and put his hands on his knees and his head down.

"Brent, honey, are you all right?"

"I'm fine. It's just lack of sleep, and I'm probably a little dehydrated."

"You're completely wet!" Brent had broken into a sweat. "Come, lay down on the couch."

The cat twisted around Angela's legs, mewing for her dinner, indifferent to her master's suffering. Angela took Brent's jacket and led him to the couch. Brent lay down and Angela went into the kitchen to get him some water.

She handed him the water. "Are you feeling better?"

Brent propped his head up and sipped at the water. "A little, thanks."

"I'll fix us something to eat. You just have to get some sleep tonight."

"First, I have to figure out what to do about tomorrow. If only Charles Stinson were alive, I could ask his advice."

"First, you have to have something to eat and get a good night's rest, or you'll be joining Charles Stinson."

"I can't take these defense cases anymore, Angie. That was never the plan, and they take too much out of me."

"Okay, let's take a break from the law; at least for dinner. We can talk about it after."


\*\*\*


It was 3 a.m. before Brent drifted to sleep. He kept closing his eyes and trying to relax, but he couldn't stop thinking ... thinking about shooting Dusty Clairborne. And when he finally did sleep, Clairborne haunted him in his dreams as surely as he had his victims, in life.

Brent drifted in and out of a shallow sleep, full of visions of Clairborne stalking and stabbing his victims. He dreamed of confronting Clairborne, over and over again. In some versions of the dream, Clairborne attacked him with the knife before he could fire a shot. In others, Clairborne hacked at him with the K-Bar. At 6 a.m., Brent finally quit fighting with his psyche. He was awake and there was nothing he could do about it.

Angela made a generous breakfast of fried eggs and potatoes to give Brent energy for the ordeal that lie ahead. The nagging question of whether to put Banks on the witness stand was still gnawing at him as he dressed for court.

\*\*\*

Judge Carlyle looked in a jovial mood when she took the bench. The trial had not been boring, but she knew that it was nearing the end and was looking forward to that. She called the court to order and Brent, Chernow and Banks stood for the jury as they filed in.

"Mr. Marks, do you have anything further to present?"

"Yes, Your Honor. I call Father Thaddeus Brown."

Father Brown took the oath and sat in the witness chair.

"Father Brown, please tell the jury about your background and experience."

"I have been a Catholic priest for over 50 years. I hold an M.S. in Psychology from Harvard and a PhD in Theology and Religious Studies from Oxford University. I am also a licensed clinical psychologist."

"Father Brown, have you counseled many individuals as a psychologist during your career?"

"Oh, yes. As a psychologist and a priest, I have counseled thousands of individuals."

"And did you have the occasion to consult with my client, Joshua Banks?"

"Yes, I have."

"As therapeutic counseler, or for a psychological evaluation?"

"I evaluated Mr. Banks at your request."

"And, as a result of your evaluation of Mr. Banks, were you able to reach an opinion, with a reasonable degree of psychological certainty, as to whether he is suffering from any psychological condition?"

"Yes. I determined that Mr. Banks suffers from obsessive-compulsive disorder of the religious subtype."

"Can you please describe this disorder, Father?"

"Certainly. Obsessive compulsive disorder is a type of anxiety disorder which involves obsessive, worrisome thoughts that an individual with the disorder seeks to deal with through compulsions, such as excessive hand washing or other rituals. In the religious subtype, these worries are about sin, and the compulsive behavior involves excessive prayer, hypermorality and cleaning rituals. He is also a hoarder, which is a typical symptom of OCD; but in his case, he can't throw away anything associated with religion. He saves bibles, bible study materials, and religious symbols."

"How does Mr. Banks' obsessive compulsive disorder manifest itself?"

"Mr. Banks is obsessed with God and terrified of committing sins. He compensates for his obsessions with hypermoral thoughts, excessive prayer, and excessive bible study. He has memorized thousands of verses from the new and old testaments, and recites them as part of his everyday speech."

On cross-examination, Chernow sought to destroy the vision Father Brown had painted of Banks.

"Father Brown, isn't it true that one of the symptoms of OCD can be obsessive violent thoughts, such as stabbing a loved one?"

"That is one subtype of OCD, yes. It's called 'harm OCD'."

"And isn't it also true that people diagnosed with OCD can suffer anger attacks which manifest themselves in aggressive behavior and threats toward others?"

"There are studies which so report, yes."

"Thank you, Father. No further questions, Your Honor."

"Mr. Marks?"

"Thank you, Your Honor. Father Brown, there are many subtypes of OCD, are there not?"

"Yes."

"And, in your evaluation of Mr. Banks, did you conclude that he suffered from the subtype, harm OCD?"

"No."

"Thank you."

# CHAPTER FORTY EIGHT

Now that Father Brown had paved the way, Brent offered Joshua Banks as a witness. He knew that Chernow would use Banks' homophobia to convince the jury of his guilt during cross-examination, but the more Brent thought about it, the more he just couldn't see putting the case to the jury with the loose end of the bloody clothes hanging over it. There had to be an explanation for that, and Banks was the only one who could provide it.

Banks walked up to the witness stand like a little kid who had been caught shoplifting. *He looks guilty before he even opens his mouth!* Brent had counseled him well on taking the affirmation to tell the truth, and he passed without any emotional outbursts. *Here goes...*

335

Banks was stiff, and looked intently toward Brent, anticipating his question. He avoided looking at the jury.

"Mr. Banks, you know why you're here in court, don't you?"

"Yes, I do. God is putting me to a test."

"Mr. Banks, did you kill Ronald and James Bennett?"

"No! No! As God is my witness, I did not! I could not!"

"But you did throw a rock through their window, didn't you?"

Banks hung his head in shame. "Yes, I did that. It was a sin, a terrible sin."

"Mr. Banks, after your arraignment in this case, do you remember being on the Sheriff's bus?"

"Yes, I remember."

"What happened to you on that bus?"

"A demon appeared: a most vile and disgusting creature."

"Mr. Banks, are you saying that you saw a demon?"

"Yes, an unclean spirit, who appeared to me in the guise of an angel."

Brent did not anticipate the demon talk to come out so quickly, so he approached Banks with a photograph of Clairborne.

"Mr. Banks, can you identify the person in this picture?"

"That is no person, Mr. Marks. That is the demon, in his human form. I *saw* him."

"You say he came to you as an angel. Did he take you out of the bus?"

"Yes, he did. I thought he was trying to save me, but he had no such intention."

"What happened to everyone else on the bus?"

Banks began to cry. "The demon slaughtered them!"

"Did you see him kill them?"

"No, I was asleep. But I heard their cries in my dreams."

*God, did I make a mistake calling him? He's completely departed from the coaching I gave him.*

Brent ran with it. "Did you see the truck hit the bus?"

"No, but I heard a terrible crash. Like thunder from the depths of hell."

"And were you injured?"

"I was unconscious."

"Did you awaken?"

"Yes."

"How?"

"The demon lifted me out."

"How did you know that everyone else had been killed?"

Banks wailed. "God, I saw the blood, the bodies, as the demon carried me out!"

"And where did the demon take you?"

"I don't know where."

"Did he hold you as his prisoner?"

"Yes! He locked me away. No food, no water for days."

"Did you finally escape from the demon?"

"Yes."

"How?"

"God helped me. And he sent me you, Mr. Marks."

"How did God help you?"

"I awoke, and looked around. The room was spinning. I was dizzy. The demon was nowhere to be found, so I saw my chance to escape. The doors were unlocked."

"Did you leave?"

"I couldn't. I was naked."

"What did you do?"

"I looked for clothes. I didn't know where I was or what was happening, but I knew I needed clothes."

"Were you able to find your own clothes?"

"No, no. I found some clothes the demon had left behind, and put them on."

"Then what did you do?"

"I ran."

# CHAPTER FORTY NINE

Chernow's objective in cross-examination was to push Banks' buttons, and he started pushing right away.

"Mr. Banks, you testified that you threw the rock through James and Ronald Bennett's window, is that correct?"

"Yes, I did. And God has forgiven me for that."

"Does God forgive all sins?"

"Yes, he does."

"Would God forgive you of murder?"

"Through our Lord, Jesus Christ, all sins of the believer are forgiven."

"Even murder?"

"Even murder."

"And you are a believer in Christ, correct?"

"Yes, sir, I am."

"You threw the rock at the Bennett's window because they were gay, isn't that correct?"

"Yes."

"And homosexuality is a sin, isn't it?"

"Yes."

"It is a sin punishable by death, isn't it?"

"Yes."

"You know that because it's in the Bible, isn't it?"

"Yes."

"Where is it in the Bible, Mr. Banks?"

Banks stood up. The judge turned her head and raised her voice. "Mr. Banks, sit down." Banks looked at the judge like he had been caught with his hand in the cookie jar. He sat down slowly.

"Where is it in the Bible, Mr. Banks?"

Banks pointed his finger upwards, as if it was an antenna to God. "Leviticus 20:13 says: 'If a man also lie with mankind, as he lieth with a woman, both of them have committed an abomination: they shall surely be put to death; their blood shall be upon them!'"

"And you told this to Ronald and James Bennett outside of court in the case concerning their same-sex marriage, didn't you?"

"Yes, I did."

"You are a servant of God, aren't you, Mr. Banks?"

"Yes, I am."

Chernow rose from the counsel table and approached Banks with the photograph of Dusty Clairborne.

"You testified that this was the demon you saw in the bus, correct?"

"Yes, yes, that's him."

"Is this the first photograph you ever saw of him?"

"Yes."

"Is this exactly the way you remember him?"

"Well, not exactly."

"Not exactly? Exactly what did this demon look like, Mr. Banks?"

"He was foul-smelling, and had a thousand eyes protruding from his skin."

Chernow looked at the jury and repeated the answer. "A thousand eyes?"

"Yes."

"What else did he have, Mr. Banks?"

"He had horns growing from his head."

Chernow looked back at the jury, with skepticism. "Horns growing from his head?"

"Yes."

"Mr. Banks, when you threw that rock, you wanted to punish James and Ronald Bennett, didn't you?"

"Yes."

"That was a sin, wasn't it?"

Banks cried again. "Yes! Yes!"

"And you were forgiven for that sin?"

"Yes."

"But the punishment for their sins was death, wasn't it?"

"Yes."

"And that's what they got, isn't it, Mr. Banks?"

Banks looked confused.

"Objection, argumentative!"

"Overruled. The witness may answer."

"That's what they got, didn't they, Mr. Banks? Death!"

"Yes."

"And you delivered that punishment, didn't you?"

"No! No!"

Banks stood up again.

"Sit down Mr. Banks, or the Bailiff will restrain you."

"I didn't!"

"Sit down, Mr. Banks."

"But God will forgive you for killing Ronald and James Bennett, won't he?"

"Objection, argumentative!"

"Overruled."

"No, no, the demon did it!"

"The demon was inside you, wasn't it, Mr. Banks?"

"No! No! No!" Banks broke down and cried, his head in his hands. "It was the demon!"

# CHAPTER FIFTY

A confident Bradley Chernow approached the jury for his final argument. He put his hands on the railing and looked every juror in the eye.

"Ladies and gentlemen, the State of California and the County of Santa Barbara thanks you for your jury service. It is one of the most important obligations we have as citizens, and you have performed your duty well. After the judge instructs you on the law to apply to this case, you will be charged with making a most important decision.

"We all have heard about man's inner demons. But this is figurative speech; symbolic. The defendant, Joshua Banks, actually claims to see them. And he uses this demon as an excuse for his own murderous sins."

Chernow looked at the jury, then glared at Banks, who was having difficulty sitting still.

"The evidence, in this case, leads to no other reasonable interpretation. The defendant expressed his hatred toward and had already committed a violent act against the victims. You've heard from his own mouth that homosexuality is punishable by death. And you heard him admit that he warned the victims that death would be their punishment.

"The evidence shows, ladies and gentlemen, that the defendant is the only person who had a motive to kill Ronald and James Bennett. He was found wearing clothes stained in their blood! Yes, ladies and gentlemen, the blood of Ronald and James Bennett was on the defendant's hands!

"Mr. Marks will try to convince you that somebody else was responsible for this crime. But there is no evidence that directly links Dusty Clairborne to these murders. Was he the driver of the hit and run tow truck? There is no evidence of that. It is a smokescreen, meant to instill doubt in your minds."

Chernow carefully and methodically laid out all the evidence in his case. During his presentation, the jury paid attention. If they were working on their shopping lists or thinking about their favorite TV shows, it was not evident from their expressions.

"Ladies and gentlemen, the evidence in this case points to one perpetrator, and one alone; and that is Joshua Banks, the defendant..."

Chernow pointed his finger at Banks, who cowered at counsel table.

"It was Joshua Banks, whether he was the demon or the demon was inside him, who committed this horrific murder, with a knife. It was he who decided to execute them for what he perceived to be their sins, punishable by death, and this, the People have proven beyond a reasonable doubt. Your duty, ladies and gentlemen, is to return a verdict of guilty as charged."

Chernow returned to his seat, and the judge checked the clock.

"It's about time for the lunch break. We will recess now until 1:30. Mr. Marks, please be prepared to give your argument at that time."

*\*\*\**

Brent mustered up all his energy for this final argument. He had doubts as to whether putting Banks on the stand was the right thing to have done, but it was too late now. He confidently stood in front of the jury and made eye contact with each one of them.

"Ladies and gentlemen, this is the stage of the trial where the lawyers get a chance to persuade you. Mr. Chernow has made a very persuasive argument, but it is not the arguments that you are to consider in this case. You may consider only the evidence. And you must look at every piece of evidence through the looking glass of reasonable doubt."

Brent moved close to the jury, and put his hand on the balustrade of the box as he paced and outlined every element of the crime, emphasizing that the prosecution had not proven them beyond a reasonable doubt.

"This is a case of circumstantial evidence. Are Joshua Banks' religious beliefs that homosexuality is a sin sufficient to infer that he is guilty of these murders? No! He admits throwing the rock at the window, expresses remorse for it, but does not admit that he committed these murders. The prosecution did not find the knife. *We* did. The exact type of

350

knife used in the murders was found in the possession of Dusty Clairborne, who was the primary suspect in the theft of the tow truck.

"And what about the so-called hit and run accident? Joshua Banks' leg was shackled to the frame of the bus. His hands were handcuffed and his torso chained. It was virtually impossible for him to get out of those restraints without aid. The prosecution has no explanation for how this happened. They want you to believe that the bus was struck by a hit and run driver and that somehow Joshua was able to not only survive the crash, but also slip out of all those restraints and escape. Surely common sense tells us that this couldn't happen by magic. Joshua didn't say abracadabra and *poof!* his chains disappeared."

Despite the seriousness of the subject, the men on the jury were smiling at this comment.

"No, ladies and gentlemen, there is no evidence as to how he was able to free himself from these restraints, except for his own explanation: Dusty Clairborne, the demon personified. The only reasonable inference to draw from the facts is that Dusty Clairborne drove that tow truck into the Sheriff's bus and killed everyone on board except for Joshua Banks, whom he kept prisoner, as his patsy. He drugged him with PCP to keep him at bay and then, when the time was right, discarded him as

351

his fall guy. He knew there was no physical evidence connecting Joshua with this crime, so he made sure that Joshua would do the only logical thing when he started to wake up from his drugged stupor and had the urge to run. He provided the bloody clothes that Joshua needed to wear – which also served as the frameup for this crime. And what about the clothes? They don't fit! They are Dusty Clairborne's size, not Joshua's.

"The People have failed to satisfy their burden of proving every element of this case beyond a reasonable doubt, and you have the duty to return with a verdict of acquittal."

Chernow was allowed to have the last word, and he did not waste that opportunity.

"Ladies and gentlemen, at the conclusion of the People's case, it should have been very clear to each one of you that the People have proven every element of murder in the first degree beyond a reasonable doubt. Nobody had a motive to kill James and Ronald Bennett except for the defendant. He threatened them with death in front of dozens of witnesses, then he carried out that threat in cold blood, stabbing the life out of each of them over twenty times."

Chernow slapped his hand on the balustrade. "Twenty times! And this motive is connected with the physical evidence, ladies and gentlemen: the clothes that Joshua Banks was wearing were stained with the blood of the victims. Given these facts, there can be no reasonable doubt that it was the defendant who killed Ronald and James Bennett in cold blood, and your duty is to render a verdict of guilty."

The final battle was now over, and the judge gave instructions to the jury on the law to apply to the evidence they had heard, and sent them off to deliberate. Brent was so exhausted that he almost nodded off in his chair during the recitation, which took a little over an hour.

# CHAPTER FIFTY ONE

Brent made it home just in time for the call from Melinda that the jury had reached a verdict, and it would be announced the next morning in court. *Not a good sign. An early jury verdict usually means a guilty verdict.* Brent sweated over the verdict all night in his third night of no sleep. The sleeping pill he took put him out for the first two hours, and after that he spent the night tossing, turning, and thinking. Drifting in and out of sleep, he dreamed of shooting Clairborne, saw each the blood spurting from each bullet hole in slow motion, and watched his head explode. Brent finally decided to relieve his tortured soul from the job of trying to sleep and got up.

Judge Carlyle called court to session and the jury took their places.

"I understand that the jury has reached a verdict."

"Yes, Your Honor." The white, retired postal worker stood up with the verdict in hand.

"The foreman will hand the Clerk the verdict."

The foreman handed the paper to the Clerk.

"The Clerk will publish the verdict."

"We the jury in the above-entitled cause find the defendant, Joshua Banks, guilty of murder in the first degree of James Bennett as charged in Count I of the indictment, and further find him guilty of murder in the first degree of Ronald Bennett, as charged in Count II of the indictment."

Susan Fredericks raised her arm in a gesture of victory, and glared at Brent.

"What's happened? What's going on?" Joshua Banks looked to the left and right, disoriented, as the Bailiff took him into custody as the game played itself out.

"We've lost, Mr. Banks. I'm terribly sorry."

"Lost? How could we lose? It wasn't me! It was the demon! The demon!"

The Bailiff led Banks out of the room.

"Tough break, Marks." Bradley Chernow extended his hand. Brent took it, tentatively.

"You know that justice wasn't done here."

Brent looked into Chernow's eyes. He seemed to be fine with the outcome.

# CHAPTER FIFTY TWO

The remainder of Joshua Banks' ordeal was no surprise, given the guilty verdict. Judge Carlyle denied Brent's motion for a new trial. She couldn't risk granting it in an election year. After that, the penalty phase of the trial went forward. The jury's choices were limited: death, or life without the possibility of parole. The jury chose death. Joshua Banks' fate would be sealed as soon as the California Supreme Court decided his automatic appeal; a process which would take many years. In the meantime, he would sit on death row.

Banks' court-appointed counsel filed a petition for writ of habeas corpus in state court, alleging that the prosecution withheld evidence that could have been exculpatory. It also alleged that Brent had provided ineffective assistance as counsel. The Honeymoon Stalker case was reopened when DNA belonging to one of the other victims had been found on the handle of Clairborne's knife. This closed the book on the other cases, but never caused a ripple in the Banks case. Brent could only hope that this new DNA evidence would make a difference on appeal, and that, when all had been said and done, justice would finally prevail.

# EPILOGUE

Brent had vowed not to take on any more criminal cases. The pressure of the Banks case and the shooting of Dusty Clairborne had taken too much out of him. He was disillusioned with the entire justice system and especially critical of his role in it. He wondered if he had screwed up and thought over and over again how he could have done it differently. Maybe it was a mistake to have Banks testify. The unanswered questions loomed over him and tortured him day and night.

After the case, Brent took a long sabbatical. He kept Melinda on at the office, referring cases to other attorneys as they came in, from time to time. Brent spent most of his days sitting on the balcony, reading a book or watching the ebb and flow of the tides, the setting of the sun, and the rising of the moon. Life went on all around him, but he was stuck at this moment in his own life, thinking and pondering all his decisions up to this point. *What would Charles Stinson say about all this?*

"Brent, Father Brown's here." Angela called out to Brent, who was sitting on the balcony having a drink and looking at the harbor.

"Show him in!"

Father Brown hung up his jacket and Brent invited him to sit down on the terrace with him. The sun was sifting through the clouds, its rays streaming through the clouds to Earth.

"It's beautiful out here."

"Yes, it is. Can I offer you a drink, Father?"

"Only if you insist."

Brent poured Father Brown a generous portion of Napa Valley Cabernet.

"I hope this isn't a habit of yours."

"Sitting on the balcony in the fresh air, or drinking wine?"

"Neither. Stepping away from the law, is what I meant."

"The law is unfair, Father."

"Of course it's unfair. The law is a creation of man, Brent. Only God is perfect. Man is fallible. Just look at all that is going on in the world now. Our Father in Heaven is probably looking down at us and shaking his holy head right now. But he's mostly disappointed with you, Brent."

"With me?"

"Yes. Nobody says that what you do is easy. That's why not just anyone can do it. You're the champion of the weak, the oppressed – everyone whom Jesus Christ nurtured and protected."

"I just can't do it anymore, Father. It's too discouraging."

"What did your mentor, Charles Stinson, always used to say about that?"

"I've forgotten, Father. I wish he were here."

"He is here. Here," Father Brown said, pointing to Brent's head. "And here," pointing to his heart. "What would be his advice to you?"

Brent thought for a moment. *What would he be saying if Charles was standing right here, in front of me?* Suddenly, he realized what he would say.

"To get back out there and give 'em hell. Oops, excuse me, Father."

"That's right. So you get back in there and give 'em - well, give 'em hell, just like he said."

Father Brown smiled, and the smile did not waiver until Brent acknowledged it with his own weak smile. Father Brown stood up.

"Now that I've delivered the message, I think I can go on to the next mission."

Brent rose and shook his hand. "Me too, Father."

# AFTERWORD

As with all my novels, "Absolute Intolerance" is a story with a higher purpose. In this case, it is an expose on hate and homophobia. According to the FBI National Press Office, as of 2010, 19.3% of hate crimes in the United States were motivated by sexual orientation bias. According to a 2010 Intelligence Report by the Southern Poverty Law Center, LGBT people are far more likely to be the subject of a hate crime than any other minority group in America.

I thought it would be interesting to examine two different types of aberrant behavior and find out what happens when homophobia intersectrs with serial killing, and give the lawyer/protagonist the moral quandary of having to decide whether or not to defend the religious fanatic accused of murdering his former clients.

In the end, if we are to survive as a country, we have to remember that tolerance is the most important concept for peaceful living in our society. Live and let live. Love and let love. It is only by realizing this that we can live in peace together.

Reviews are the mainstay of any author, and are much appreciated. Finally, I love to get email from my readers; even if it is an error that you noticed that perhaps my editors, beta readers, or I did not catch. I want to make sure that my books are as high-quality as possible for my readers.

Please feel free to send me your comments, to: info@kennetheade.com. I also invite you to join my mailing list for advance notice of new books, free excerpts, free books, and updates. I will never spam you. Please subscribe here: http://bit.do/mailing-list.

**One more thing…**

If you believe your friends would enjoy this book, I would be honored if you would post your thoughts and also leave a review on Amazon.

Best regards,

Kenneth Eade

info@kennetheade.com

## **BONUS OFFER**

Sign up for paperback discounts, advance sale notifications of this and other books, and free stuff at: http://bit.do/mailing-list. I will never spam you.

# ABOUT THE AUTHOR

Author Kenneth Eade, best known for his legal and political thrillers, practiced law for 30 years before publishing his first novel, "An Involuntary Spy." Eade, an up-and-coming author in the legal thriller and courtroom drama genre, has been described by critics as "one of our strongest thriller writers on the scene, and the fact that he draws his stories from the contemporary philosophical landscape is very much to his credit." Critics have also said that "his novels will remind readers of John Grisham, proving that Kenneth Eade deserves to be on the same lists with the world's greatest thriller authors."

Says Eade of the comparisons: "John Grisham is famous for saying that sometimes he likes to wrap a good story around an important issue. In all of my novels, the story and the important issues are always present."

Eade is known to keep in touch with his readers, offering free gifts and discounts to all those who sign up at his web site, www.kennetheade.com.

Made in the USA
Lexington, KY
08 January 2016